TENINO CAVERNS

HIDDEN MOUNTAIN CHRONICLES
BOOK 3

PATRICK TALMADGE

HANGAR 1 PUBLISHING

CONTENTS

BACK STORY

In 1912 the Hercules Sandstone Co. set off one of the biggest blasts in history. The record explosion was in the city of Tenino, Washington. They accomplished it with 50,000 pounds of dynamite and black powder. The blast was to break up 500,000 tons of sandstone. The whole city of Tenino and people from towns around the state and country came to watch the great blast. What no one knew was that a stranger was in town to watch the blast and assess his theory of ground echoing.

His name was Ruston Packwood and he believed you could map the earth to great depths using the vibrations from an earthquake. When he heard of the great blast that the Hercules Sandstone Co. was going to do, he knew it was his chance to evaluate his theory without waiting for an unpredictable earthquake. Ruston had put his listening bells all over the Tenino valley and up four of the deeper ravines on each side. He was extremely interested in the old volcanic lake from which Scatter Creek flowed. He was curious what had caused the side of the crater to give way and create Lake Mcintosh. He was hoping his theory could shed light on that and why there was so much sandstone in this valley.

When Ruston Packwood examined the first reading from the

blast, he was speechless. The first bell he checked had printed a perfect map of the ground beneath them. Once he was able to piece all of them together, he would have a map of the ground beneath Tenino and hopefully the location of any gold, silver, oil, or coal in it. If he were right, money would soon be no problem.

After three weeks of demanding work going over a dozen rechecks Ruston had his map, and it was nothing like he ever expected. Sure, he could see what he thought was oil and coal that he could make good money selling the location information, but there was no money to make from gold or silver because there was not any to speak of. It was that huge void about three and a half miles below the surface that had caused Ruston to check and recheck his results so many times.

Ruston Packwood had been a geologist for over 40 years, and he could not explain that thing below. His best guess was a cavern. The bells kept moving as if the thing below was hollow and ringing from the explosion, even days afterwards. If it was a cavern, then the two shaft like shapes jutting out from it to the surface could be openings into it. Ruston knew one was near the old volcano caldera, but his bells were not close enough to see exactly where it hit the surface. Even though his bells had not found where the second shaft ended, it went near the Tenino Sandstone Company quarry on the south end of town up against the hill. Ruston went to speak with the owner of the Tenino Sandstone Co. and see if he could make a deal.

No one knows for sure what deal Ruston made, but in 1914 three of the quarry workers spoke of a special dig going on at the bottom of the quarry. Strange workers showed up and built a small building at the bottom of the quarry up against the south wall. For the next 3 years, digging material came out of the small building as more drilling equipment went inside. No quarry workers were permitted inside the small building. It was obvious they said drilling was going on and drilling deep it was. The workers said they would bet they were drilling for oil after the big oil bust a couple of years back. The secret operation continued until the 1930's. No one ever found out what was going on in that building. Before anyone could learn the real story, the quarry flooded.

The legends say two boys were walking by the Quarry late one night and heard yelling from the quarry. When the boys got to the quarry it was full of water and had become a large pond. In the center of the pond was the man who was doing all the yelling. The boys threw pieces of wood towards the man until he was able to grab one and swim to the edge using it as a float. Once they had him out of the water the boys could not understand what the man was saying. He seemed quite hysterical and kept saying "they told us that we were not supposed to be there. They chased me away and no one else made it out."

For ten minutes they tried to calm him down. Then suddenly he stood up, walked to a truck, and drove away, or so the legend says. To this day no one knows anything of the man, the secret drilling operation, and why the quarry filled with water that night. The quarry road closed, and eventually they would make a swimming pool out of it, not knowing what was really at the bottom. Only the unidentified man that left that night and the men lost at the bottom know for sure.

1

WHERE IS GRANDPA

While changing filthy clothes in the back hall Raymond complained aloud about the oily black dirt from the back field that had ruined all his clothes. After making half a dozen comments about the dirt, he heard a voice from the living room. What do you expect from an old oil exploration drill hole young man?

Raymond excitedly called out, "is that you Junior?" "Who else would it be, silly?" As fast as he could, Raymond stripped out of his dirty clothes into clean ones. While coming out of the utility room, he was asking Junior how long he had been there, how long can he stay, and why didn't he call him in from the field? Smiling as he talked, Junior answered all his questions, then added he did not call him in, because it was too much fun watching him get so dirty. With a snort, Raymond grabbed Junior, hugged him, looked him in the eye and asked, "what do you mean by an old oil exploration drill hole? One look told Junior Raymond wasn't lying and knew nothing of the drill hole. Junior looked at Grandma Werner sitting quietly as usual in her chair facing the field. He asked, "mom didn't you ever tell Raymond about the drill hole, and how dad went missing?" Grandma Werner sat still for quite a while. Junior was about to ask her a second time when she turned away from the window towards them. When she spoke, Grandma sounded different than Raymond had ever heard her speak. She sounded like she was much younger and clear headed. Usually, Grandma does not speak, and when she does, all 107 years of her age comes through. Right now, she was speaking like a young lady reading a story.

Grandma looked at Raymond and smiled. "Young man when you and Stella moved in over twenty years ago to take care of me, I was mad," she said. "You upset my life. People said I wasted my life waiting for a man who never came back. Do not look so surprised, I am not brain dead, I just did not want to talk to you. Raymond, you are the one who brought me out of my self-pity. I watched you work in the back field and play with your dogs. You looked just like my Papa when he was young. He even had a German Shepard like you. My heart softened as I watched you and Stella live the life I had dreamed of with my Papa. As the years passed, I dreamed of my Papa being with me again. I lived the life I prayed for even though it was in my dreams. I long ago gave up hope Papa would return to me, but used these years to relive memories, and dream of what could have been. I am a happy woman these days and made amends to God for taking him away."

Let me tell you a bit about Papa that you may not know. Like you Raymond, he could not stay seated and had to tinker. He made a small fortune during the Tenino oil rush days because he was handy. What set him up for life was when he told a man he had just met the truth. Papa was working on the oil drilling rigs in town and when he was having a beer at the tavern, he struck up a conversation with a man who was interested in investing in the oil drilling operations. The man was in town to buy stock. Papa later told me he liked the man the moment he spoke to him. The man was also an inventor and was building planes up North in Seattle. They had talked inventions, and new gadgets for quite a while, then the man spoke about stock investment in oil. Papa told me he decided to tell the man what he thought about investing in oil. The man listened to Papa closely. After

Papa finished, the man thanked him and offered him a job on the spot in his factory making planes in Seattle at the Boeing plant.

Papa had saved Bill Boeing money because the oil never panned out in Tenino. Bill was grateful and gave Papa a job in design engineering. Best thing was, Papa could work his own hours. Papa and Bill had a wonderful friendship. That was 1914 and two years later Bill's airplane business took off. Over the years Bill had become too busy to visit every week like in the past, but at least once a month he would come by. That is probably where Papa went for help when he found the rocks, she said. Junior asked softly as if not to ruin the mood, if Grandma still had the rock. Grandma smiled, and said, "always my dear boy." She looked at Raymond, and asked him to move the curtain behind the chair she was sitting in. In all the years Raymond had lived in the house he had never thought much about the small curtain or thought about what was behind it. Mostly because Grandma was always sitting there. Once Raymond opened the curtain, you could see a small nook with a tea cart inside. "Please roll that cart out to me Raymond," she asked with a smile.

When he pulled on the cart Raymond could barely budge it. Raymond thought it had sat there so long that the tires had frozen to the floor. Grandma suggested the cart might be a bit heavier than expected, and a bit more effort might move it. With a red face Raymond used both hands and began to pull the cart out. Still, it took quite a bit of effort to move the cart. As it rolled out, Raymond could see the cart was metal with large tires. The cart had not moved for years, yet it moved across that hardwood floor smoothly with enough effort. Once the cart was in front of Grandma, the room fell silent. I was the only one who had never heard of the rock on the cart, and they were all waiting for me to hear the story.

Grandma said, "before I bought this house, Papa and I lived two blocks away by the high school. Papa used to walk over here, and go up the mountain to pick berries, mushrooms, and get away to think with his dog. He never let anyone know where his favorite spot was, but he always came back with full buckets. One day Papa came back all excited about a rock that he had been sitting on for years, which had been turned over by a tree that fell over. The tree blew over, and exposed the underside of the rock, and ten loose pieces that had broken off. He said it was too heavy to carry a big piece, so he only brought a small piece back with him. He was going to get Uncle Kurt to help him get every piece they could and find where that rock came from. He also wanted to explore the strange cave he found nearby, where he found the rock.

I was looking at this man I loved, who sounded like a babbling fool talking about a rock. Papa saw the look on my face and started laughing. He said, okay my love, let me show you a small piece of what has gotten me so excited. If I am right these rocks will make us very wealthy. With that Papa pulled this small quarter sized rock from a pouch and handed it to me. I almost dropped it Grandma said because it was so heavy. It must have weighed two or three pounds, and it was tiny. I looked at Papa and asked him if it was gold. He said he did not know for sure if it was gold, because it was much heavier than gold. He thought it was rarer than gold because it was a clear crystal. He wanted to get the rest of the rocks, then find out for sure.

I looked at the stone, then at Papa, and knew he was going to do it regardless of what I thought. I smiled at Papa and reminded him that the kids and I were heading to Hoquiam to see my sister for two weeks. At least he should have time to collect his silly rocks. I assured him I was fine with the money we had, but if they were worth money could I have a new car? Papa smiled knowing I was ok with his plans and promised a new car if they made money. Papa spent the rest of the day planning with Kurt. By bedtime we kissed good night, and that was the last time I saw him. Papa woke up early, kissed me on the cheek, and was gone. I left for my sisters and when I got home two weeks later, I found this cart just inside the door. I was carrying a box through the door and tripped over the cart. I went over the cart and fell to the floor. The heavy cart made a crashing sound, and the rock fell over. "Thank God it did not fall off the cart, or I would never have gotten it back on," Grandma said. She looked at the rock and said, "I know it is heavy, and valuable, but it was not worth losing my Papa."

Weeks later I heard men had dug a well on this property looking for something. I was wondering if it was my Papa's secret cave. I also heard the story about a man found swimming in the flooded quarry, and the drilling they were doing there. The owners deserted this property, and their drilling operation never finished. I bet the people that had drilled here had drilled at the quarry. I bought this property and have waited here since to see if my Papa would return.

Grandma sat silent for a while, then looked at Raymond. In a quiet voice she said, "Would you please find out what happened to my Papa. I know he is gone but I would like to know what happened to him. Raymond, please take that rock and sell it, to help you find Papa." Grandma then stood, gave a stunned Raymond a hug, and said it was time for a nap. Stella and her mother Carol walked Grandma to her room for a nap. There seemed to be a lightness to Grandmas' step that was not there before. Hope is a gift I can give her, Raymond thought. Junior touched him on the shoulder and asked him to go outside with him.

2

JUNIOR'S SIDE OF THE STORY

J unior went out the front door and walked down the driveway in silence. Raymond followed wordlessly knowing something was on Junior's mind, and thought it was wise to keep quiet. When they reached the road, Junior turned and walked towards the Scatter Creek bridge three hundred feet away. Once they reached the middle of Scatter Creek bridge Junior stopped, leaned against the railing, and silently stared into the trees. Grandma was wrong about no one knowing Papa's secret spot. When I was eight years old, I awoke one morning before light as Papa was about to leave for his secret spot to hunt mushrooms. Out of curiosity I dressed and followed him. He walked from the old house over this old bridge into the woods. After 20 minutes of walking Papa slowed down along a cliff, then disappeared. It was mostly dark in the woods, but I was sure he had walked through a rock wall. When I got to that spot all I saw was a small marsh with a rock wall behind it. No sign of Papa. I began to wonder if he had fallen into the marsh, when he stepped out from the wall and smiled at me. "Hey Junior," he called, "I had not expected you to follow me into the dark woods. Your reward is you get to be the first to see my secret spot.

Papa showed me the hidden stones just below the surface of the dark marsh water. "All you need to do is take a stick and swing it back and forth in the marsh until you find the stones," he said. "You stand on the shore facing this lighter stone above my head," Papa said. Pointing to the light-colored rock above him, he said, "start probing the water until you find the first stone." I picked up a stick and began swinging it through the water. To my surprise, I hit something right away. Feeling it carefully with my stick showed it was about the size of a dinner plate, and only an inch below the surface. I stepped on it then felt for the next until I reached Papa. We laughed and he took me to see the opening behind the rocks.

It was an exceedingly small valley, or more a cleft in the rocks about forty feet wide, and four hundred feet long. The temperature seemed warmer and there was no wind. It was a wonderful place, and I could see why Papa kept it secret, but proud Papa shared it with me. I only came up five or six times after that, and it was always special. I never told a soul until now. I even remember the tree she talked about. It was a weird bent old fruit tree that Papa said he had never seen another one like it. Junior had been looking to the East while he spoke. When he turned to Raymond, he had tears in his eyes. When Papa went missing, they shipped me off to relatives in Seattle, he said. I was not aware Papa had gone missing for a year. By then, it was too late to do anything, and I was afraid to say anything, and I was too young to know better. By the time I got older, it was too late, or so I thought until tonight.

Everyone was looking in the wrong place. Papa always said his place was a two hour walk in the woods. He always used the extra time to relax and think in that beautiful spot. So, when they went looking, they went all the way to Lake Mcintosh to look. They were miles off. Junior looked to the east again and pointed. Raymond, you walk to the end of the bridge, look due east. Hold your arm to the east, then like the hands of the clock point to 11:55 O'clock. Walk in that direction for 20 minutes, and you will find the rock wall, and the marsh if they are still there. If you see the large rock sitting all alone, and hopefully the old bent tree, you will know it is the spot. Please help Grandma but promise me you will not tell anybody what I told you until I have died. I could not live with myself if they knew. Raymond looked at Junior and hugged him. Looking into Juniors eyes, Raymond told Junior his secret was safe, and no one would blame an eight-year-old.

Raymond and Junior walked back to the house in silence. Carol was ready to leave when they got back. Everyone said their goodbyes, then Stella and Raymond went inside the house. As they passed the cart, Stella asked if he thought he could help Grandma. Raymond kept the new secret, but said he was sure he could help with his knowledge of these woods. "In fact, Stella, I know where that spot is," he said. Stella hugged Raymond and said, "I hope so for Grandma's sake." Stella went into the kitchen while Raymond took the stone into the utility room to see if he could clean it up. After Raymond got the stone into the utility room, he tried to move the rock. He could not budge it with his hands. He got a crowbar, a couple wood wedges, gloves, and set to task lifting the stone. It took four tries to get the crowbar under a corner of the rock to lift it high enough to place a wood wedge under it. After five minutes lifting with the crowbar and jacking the rock up with the wedges, Raymond could finally see a bit of the bottom. To his surprise, unlike the top, it was shiny.

While he was looking at the shiny underside of the rock Raymond saw papers under it that looked like they had writing on them. The papers looked pinned down hard by the rock. Using the crowbar and a board, he was able to lift the rock onto its edge and balance it. Once he had it balanced, Raymond used braces to hold the rock upright. Once the rock was stable Raymond used a flashlight to look at the rock. The rock looked like a Geod; dark on the outside and shiny on the inside. Except the shiny part of the rock was clear like a diamond, but with a gold tint. It was also unbelievably heavy. Heavier than even gold. Raymond did not know too much about gold but knew it was not near this heavy. He did not have any idea what type of stone it was. It was not just a dumb heavy rock now that he had seen the crystal underside. Obviously, it was rare and worth big money. With the thought of riches on his mind Raymond turned his attention to the papers he had found.

The papers had been under the rock since Grandma tripped over the cart in 1936 and knocked the rock onto them. The papers consisted of a handwritten note and two envelopes. Raymond picked up the note and read. He almost cried when he read the note. Papa had written it to Grandma. It said he and Kirk had gone into the cave to search and would be back as soon as they could. He had also taken a large stone to his friend Bill Boeing to trade for supplies needed to explore a long shaft inside the cave. The letter went on to explain, Bill loaned him two miles of stainless-steel cable, so Papa could explore the shaft. The letter also said Papa loaned a stone to Mr. Hall of the UW Museum for them to study.

Papa explained that the rocks were crystal gold, but much harder and heavier. He said the largest stones were still up at his spot, and that they were going to make them very wealthy. The envelopes contained a pair of legal documents. One was from Boeing and was the contract between Papa and Bill Boeing regarding the rock. The rock was a loan, and Papa would get it back when he returned the cable he was borrowing to explore the cavern. The other contract was from The University of Washington Museum. The contract stated that the museum was going to study and display the stone, and whenever Papa wanted it back, he could have it.

For all these years no one knew where Papa and Kirk really went or what they were really doing. For sure they did not know about the stone, *or stones,* Raymond thought. He was sure the stones were unique minerals. Whatever they are they must be worth big money for sure. The stone on the cart is about the size of an oval dinner plate and thick as a watermelon rind. The outside looked like a normal rock, with the underside smooth and slightly curved. Being clear as a piece of glass with the gold tint made it exotic looking. Raymond was musing that it looked like crystal gold and was dreaming of dollar signs as he gently laid the rock back down the way it had been for so many years. He did not want anyone seeing the rock until he had gotten to the bottom of Papa's disappearance and found out what these rocks were worth.

3

GRANDPA'S SECRET SPOT

After putting the rock back into the nook, Raymond planned to go into the woods and search for Papa's secret spot. He told Stella he was taking his dog for a walk, then headed to the barn to get things. Now that he knew Papa went to look at a cave, Raymond decided he needed lights and rope in case he found it. With his dog and a pack loaded with gear, he headed to the bridge for a trip into the woods to search for the secret spot. Once he reached the end of the Scatter Creek bridge, Raymond looked East, pointed to 11:55 O'clock, and headed into the woods. Raymond was certain he knew where Papa's spot was but decided to use Junior's method to find it for sure. For the last 22 years Raymond had hiked these woods. He saw deer and an occasional bear to keep you on your toes while hiking. The dog especially loves the woods. She runs ahead until she cannot see him then runs back. She must put in ten times the miles I do, he thought, and she ran ahead once more. Raymond enjoyed nothing more than walking in the woods. He grew up in Washington and spent much of his childhood in the woods. He never hunted but enjoyed tracking the animals in their natural environment. Time usually meant nothing when he was walking in the woods, but sure enough, after twenty minutes they arrived at the cliff with the marsh at the base.

The lighter rock Junior told him about was easy to spot, and Raymond headed over towards it. Once he was standing at the edge of the marsh in front of the lighter rock Raymond began probing the marsh with his walking stick. After two tries he found the first submerged rock. It felt like it was flat and about one foot square. The top of the rock was only two inches under the surface of the marsh. Before he tried stepping on the first stone, Raymond decided to feel for the stones from the dry shoreline. Raymond could tell the marsh was deep and there was no way to cross unless you swam without these rocks. The marsh was about twenty feet across, with dark water, and not something you would want to try swimming in. Raymond had seen this marsh before, but never thought of trying to cross it to look at the cliff. The woods around this marsh are open and easy to walk through. The cliff wall looked small and uninteresting, so there was no reason to get wet to see it. Once Raymond had found the first four of the submerged stone steps, he was ready to try crossing the marsh.

First, the backpack and all extra gear must come off. He really did not want to fall into the cold marsh, especially with a lot of gear which would certainly pull him under. Once all the gear was off, it was time to begin crossing. A successful first couple of steps made him feel confident that Junior had told him the truth. He continued crossing the marsh on the unseen stone steps without a mishap. Once on dry ground Raymond looked around to make sure it was safe, then headed back across the hidden stones to get his gear. With his gear back on, Raymond called his dog Piper to join him as he re-crossed the marsh. She showed no desire to cross the marsh. After calling her four times, he gave up trying and walked over to the wall. Once Raymond found the opening, and disappeared between the rocks, he heard Piper start crying. When he stepped back out from behind the rocks to talk to her, she ran quickly across the marsh. She never missed a submerged rock and was by Raymond's side crying like a baby in seconds. Piper's number one rule is, Raymond goes nowhere without her. With his friend safely by his side, they walked through the gap in the rock face and disappeared. When he came out the other side, he was shocked. It was indeed a small valley or large cleft with plants he had never seen before. It was also much warmer in the little valley.

The hidden place was small and did not take long to find the large rock Junior told him about. The tree next to the rock had rotted away, but the root ball that had turned the rock over was still intact. This was a unique and strange little place. Once he was standing next to the large rock, he saw the other large pieces of rock the letter spoke of, lying next to it. Using a thick fallen branch, he tried moving one of the large pieces of rock. It was larger and much heavier than the dinner plate sized one on the cart. It was so heavy even with the thick branch he could barely budge it. It was obvious he would need to find another way to get the heavy stones home. With that realization Raymond decided to search for the cave with the shaft inside.

He looked up at the rock wall and saw where the big rock had originally been. The spot it came from looked quite different from the surrounding rock wall. The rock had broken away from the wall exposing a strange bulge. More than forty feet of the bulge was visible. It was evident where the largest stone came from. The bulge angled up along the wall face. Raymond looked toward the downhill side and saw it ran straight into the end of the little valley. There was no way past the wall to search further, so he turned his attention uphill. The valley floor at that end was a gradual slope that he could easily walk up. Raymond was no geologist, but it looked to him like the little valley had formed when the side of the wall fell away from the rock face. After a bit more exploring the wall, he walked up the little valley to the end.

The incline at the end was easy to climb and Piper followed with no problem as well. Once he reached the top he turned around and followed the direction that the strange bulge went up the wall face. The bulge was not long but it seemed to point in a perfectly straight line until it disappeared back into the wall. Raymond noted the location, the direction it took, then walked up the hill to find where it went, and hopefully Papa's cave. The trees here were large, and the underbrush was not thick, so searching was not too hard. In no time he saw what looked like a dark depression on the hill and walked toward it. When he reached the depression, it became obvious he had found Papa's cave.

Coming out of the overgrown opening was a cable. The cable crossed a small ravine into the trees fifty feet away. Raymond, with Piper following, cautiously approached the cave where the cable came out of. The opening had overgrown, and he needed to cut the brush back to look in. The first thing he saw broke his heart. The cable stretched across the ravine and ended inside the cave. It appeared there must have been an accident, which caused the wooden cable supports in the cave to break. The wood for the cable supports was laying in pieces on the cave floor. Inside the cave, there was no cable. Raymond guessed there had been an accident, which broke the supports. The rest of the cable Papa borrowed must be at the bottom of the shaft. He looked around the small cave and saw a stack of something at the back. It looked like a stack of boxes. He looked closer and saw the boxes were still full of gear and supplies. There were ropes, packs, old mining lights, and food in the boxes. It was apparent they were planning to explore and never had a chance.

After carefully checking all the boxes, and searching the cave, Raymond pulled out a powerful flashlight, and approached what he thought was the shaft Papa had written about. As he approached the shaft, he could see there was obvious damage on the cave floor. The damage indicated there had been a violent accident. Deep gouges in the dirt and drag marks to the shafts edge were still visible after so many decades. The gouge marks stopped once they reached the shaft floor. The shaft floor and walls appeared to be like the clear gold tinted rocks in the little valley below, and at home on the cart. The shaft was perfectly round and smooth looking. It was also steep, so Raymond stayed back from the edge to be safe. It was impossible to believe a natural shaft could be so perfectly round and smooth. There was no way this shaft was natural, he thought. He walked back to the cave entrance and took off his pack.

If he wanted to explore further, it was time to put a climbing harness on and tie the rope off to a big tree outside the cave. With the safety gear on, he could safely get a closer look down into the shaft. He cautiously approached the shaft and looked closer at the rocks around the opening. The rocks around the opening of the shaft looked like the rocks Papa found. The smooth inside had a gold tint as well. The outer surface of the shaft was rough and looked like a normal rock. They were identical to the rocks that had broken away. Raymond held onto his climbing rope tightly as he stepped onto the shaft floor. It was a good thing he had a harness, and his rope was tight. One step on the shaft floor and he slipped like he had stepped onto ice. The slip landed him on the shaft floor hard. If not for the rope, he would have slid down the shaft because his pants also slid on the shaft floor. Now it was obvious why Papa had used a cable to explore. Piper quickly reacted when he fell and ran to his side in the shaft.

Raymond tried grabbing her, but was too slow, and she was past him in an instant. To his surprise she did not slip a bit. She was walking on the steep slick surface without any slipping. For an unknown reason, her paws did not slip like his shoes and pants. After making sure the rope was tight, and locked securely, he touched the shaft floor with his hand. His hand did not slide at all either. The surface was smooth but not slippery to his skin, unlike his shoes and pant material. Raymond was confused and intrigued. How could something so slippery not be slippery to his skin, or Piper's paw? He was still worried about her safety, so he had her go back into the cave, and made her stay. The floor was so slippery he had to pull himself back up into the cave with the rope.

Once safely out of the shaft he took his boots and socks off and went back to the shaft to try something. Sure enough, his feet did not slide when he walked barefoot on the shaft floor. The surface was too steep to walk on easily, but he would not have to worry about sliding if he wanted to explore with ropes. When he shined his flashlight down the shaft there appeared to be no bottom. He took his head-lamp off, placed it on the shaft floor, and let it go. Sure, enough it started down the shaft and quickly picked up speed. It was a bright headlamp, but in no time, its light faded into the darkness below. If there was a chance to explore the shaft, he would need to find out for sure how far down the shaft was. Papa must have checked to see how far down it was which is why he used two miles of cable. Raymond was not going to take chances and would have to find a way to check the depth. He put his socks and boots back on and finished exploring the small cave.

After checking all the boxes in the cave for notes or anything that might tell him what happened, he went back outside the cave. It was obvious there had been an accident and both Kirk and Papa had gone down the shaft with two miles of steel cable. If they had survived, and not been hurt too badly, they could have made it back up the shaft barefoot, with effort. Raymond was almost certain they had perished. The evidence would be down at the bottom of the shaft. He called Piper and they walked down into the ravine to see where the cable went. The other side was not more than fifty feet away, and with the thick tree cover, the underbrush was sparse. Once he reached the other side, he found where the cable started. The best part was there was an old dirt road on the other side he could use to haul the large pieces of the rock out.

Raymond followed the road downhill to see where it came out. The road began right off the main road into town half a mile from his driveway. He could use it to haul things in and out if he used a strong enough truck. Now confident that he could gather more of the stones it was time to head back home and plan how to get the rocks and explore the cavern. The main goal was to find out what happened to Papa and Kirk. He decided it was best not to let anyone know what he was doing, especially Grandma. Once he was able to reach the bottom of the shaft, he would have his answers and could let everyone know. Raymond looked back up the road and promised himself he would find a way.

Once he arrived home, he went into the barn, put his gear away, and began planning. The first thing needed was to gather as many of the broken rocks as possible, and the big stone too. Raymond was not rich, but needed money for going down the shaft, and finding out what happened to Papa. While he was thinking, a news broadcast about a convoy of military trucks came across the television. One of the trucks he saw was the perfect answer. It was a large six-by-six truck with a small crane. The huge wheels and six-wheel drive could easily drive up the road to where Papa had set the cables. The crane would be able to lift even the big rock. He would have to set up metal tripods to move the big rock up out of the little valley. He might be able to use the cable still attached to the tree. Before buying it, he had better talk to his wife. He needed to tell her everything he knew, and what his plans were.

4

BIG TRUCK AND BIG ROCKS

S tella listened to everything, then sat quietly before talking. She made Raymond promise to always be careful and wear safety gear while working. He smiled and said, "always my dear." He told her the first thing he needed was the special truck to take into the woods. They decided not to buy one but rent from a private party. After Stella was confident he was going to take every precaution, it was time to find a truck to rent. He also needed to find out who owned the property the road was on and who owned the property the rock was on. Raymond went online to find out everything he could. In just two minutes he found that a logging company owned the road. One call later he had their permission to use the road. He did not tell him the real reason he needed it, but once they found out he was going to clear the road to reach his destination they agreed. Turns out they were planning on logging into that area in five years, and having the road cleared would make their job easier. The property by the cave belonged to a local resident he knew.

Raymond's plan was to see if he could buy the piece of property the big rock and cave were on. Taking the rocks off their property would be illegal and he could lose everything. It was ten acres of wooded steep up and down unbuildable property, so he did not expect it to be expensive. After clearing his plans with his wife, he drove over to the owner's house to make a deal. Betty and Jim were good people and have lived in town their whole lives. Both were in their mid-seventies and did not get out much. Just as Raymond thought they were interested in selling the land. They asked if he wanted the whole forty acres they owned there, because they would never use it and all they did was pay taxes on it. The best part was that they offered to carry a contract with zero money down and small payments. Raymond was ecstatic and said yes knowing Stella would agree. No one knew about the hidden valley, and he knew it would be a wonderful place for a getaway in the future. Before he left, Betty drew up a contract and called their lawyer to get it finalized. They said their goodbyes and Raymond went home to tell Stella. She was happy about the deal, and asked Raymond to take her up to the marsh soon so she could see the little valley and cave.

With all the legal issues taken care of it was time to find the big truck. This was going to be the fun part, he thought. Driving around in an army truck the size of a semi-truck was going to be exciting. Driving it up the dirt road would not be a problem. The road had been unused for ten years, but the trees and brush that had grown would be easy to drive over. Just driving that big monster would clear a path in the first pass. The best thing about that truck was that it could drive anywhere with six-wheel drive and huge tires. Raymond called his friend Mike to see if he knew anyone who had one, he could rent. Mike had been a semi-truck driver and was a fantastic diesel mechanic. If anything broke or he needed help, Mike was the go-to guy.

When Mike heard Raymond wanted to rent a six-by-six, he started laughing and told him to come over and talk. Not sure if Mike was going to laugh at him for wanting such a big truck, or demand to know what he needed it for. Last time he visited, Mike made him drive an Army Hummer around twenty acres. It truly was a blast driving through mud, over logs and into the three-foot-deep pond. When Raymond pulled into Mike's steep dirt road, he was surprised by what he saw. Not only was there the usual army green Hummers,

Blazers, and trucks, but there was a huge new addition to the fleet. Mike had an Army green 8X8 and it had a crane. Now he knew why Mike laughed and wanted him to come over. Mike was standing on the back of the big truck with a smile and a beer as Raymond parked.

Mike stayed on the truck as he walked towards the big green monster. The first thing out of Mike's mouth was, is this big enough? All Raymond could do was smile and shake his head in disbelief. Come on up and check it out kid, said Mike. He was excited climbing up the ladder to Mike and greeted him with a hug on top. They walked around the trucks top mounting deck to check out the crane and winches. "Do you think you can use this," asked Mike? Raymond was still in shock that he had this thing and decided to tell Mike a bit about why he needed it. He told him the reason he needed it was to drive up a slightly overgrown dirt logging road to bring out big, beautiful, and very heavy rocks. That was all Mike needed to hear, and told Raymond if he needed, help just ask. After explaining where the rocks were and how they had to take them out, Mike told Raymond he could weld up four strong tripods that would work. "Sounds great to me," said Raymond. All right, the tripods will be complete tomorrow, and I will drop them off on my way to work.

Mike suggested it was time to learn how to drive the beast. It was a bit more complicated to drive than your average station wagon. After a couple of hours of practice driving and using the crane, Raymond felt comfortable enough to drive it home. Mike smiled, and said his new toy was going to do fun work. He knew Mike loved his toys and having someone using one always made him happy. Just a big boy with big toys. After thanking him for being able to borrow his eight-by-eight Raymond drove it home. Driving an army eight-by-eight truck on a public road is a unique experience. Everyone stares and you get the right of way at every intersection. The top speed is only 50 mph, but no one dared complain that it was behind. Driving it on a dirt road will be more fun because there will be no other cars, thought Raymond. Stella came out to look at the green beast. "Please tell me you will take me for a ride before you take it back," she said. "I promise," he said as he climbed down.

The next morning Mike dropped off four heavy duty tripods. He brought them in another big army truck with a winch. All Raymond could do was laugh at his crazy friend. The smaller truck was a big green army four-by-four the size of a semi-truck. The four large tripods looked strong enough to support a house. Mike said they were stainless steel and should be able to easily (lift) any rock the crane could lift or pull. After he transferred the tripods to the bigger truck Mike left for work. As he was driving away, Mike yelled, have fun, and do not get hurt Raymond. "Promise not to," he said. *Tripods would be perfect for moving the rocks,* he thought. Mike had said the crane was able to lift over thirty thousand pounds and pull even more. The rocks were heavy but hopefully not too heavy. It was 8:00 in the morning so Raymond went inside and said goodbye to Stella. He grabbed his gear and called for Piper.

Once they were in the truck, they headed up the hill to the logging road. When they got to the dirt road he pulled in and stopped. The logging company gave him a key for the lock and asked him to be sure to close and lock it once they went in. It was nice to be able to lock the gate and keep prying eyes out, not that anyone ever comes up this way. The truck mowed down the small trees and brush that had grown over the last few years with ease. The road was still in great shape with no washouts, so the drive went quickly. The tree that Papa had used was only a mile up the road, so they reached it quickly. Mike said the cable length on the crane was over three hundred feet which was twice the length of most. They had used it to pull tanks out of the mud, so it was much stronger too. Piper and Raymond got out of the truck and looked around. He planned to remove Papa's old cable from the tree and pull it across the ravine to where the truck was. He did not want to take the chance someone would see the cable and follow it to the cave. Once the old cable was down, and stored behind a tree, he felt relief.

After hiding the old cable Raymond dragged the new cable down the ravine and up the other side near the cave. He attached a pully to a big tree, strung the cable through it and drug it back to the truck. He was going to drag the tripods over by the cave with the winch.

They were heavy and he did not want to move them by hand. He only had to move three of the tripods because he needed one by the truck. Moving them with the winch was easy, and he finished in no time. Mike had rigged a remote control for the winch that Raymond could carry, so he could watch when he pulled the big rock. He set one tripod at the top of the ravine by the cave, one at the bottom of the small valley just below the ravine and one halfway to the big rock. If he were lucky the big rock would be light enough to move. The big rock was five feet long, and two feet tall and two feet wide. The smaller pieces were only two to three feet long and less than a foot thick, but he could not move them an inch by hand. Once he had the tripods set, he ran the cable through the pulleys on each one, and he was ready to start. He thought it would be better to move the smaller pieces first in case he ran into trouble with the big rock.

Mike had also included a couple nets made from winch cable to make moving the rocks easier. They were heavy to drag by hand but would make moving the rocks easier than trying to wrap the cable around them. Raymond could not lift the rocks to put the cable nets around them, so he dug the dirt out from around the smaller rocks. With the dirt gone the edge of the cable net slid under the rocks.(too many repetitive words) He knew when he turned on the winch the cable would slide under the rocks and into the net. Raymond hooked one of the nets to the cable and started the winch moving slowly. As expected, the cable slid under the rock and into the net. It moved easier than Raymond thought, so he hooked the cable up to the second small rock and pulled the net around it. Both rocks moved so easily he decided to pull the third rock as well. When he had all three rocks at the top of the ravine by the cave, he took a deep breath and relaxed. After the rocks were safely on the truck, he set his sights on the big rock. There were ten or more smaller pieces ranging in size from an egg to grapefruits that he could easily move later without the crane. He wanted to take those smaller pieces home and hide them in the chance something happened to the ones he finished loading.

Now the time came to try the big rock. Raymond drug the cable back down the ravine and up to the cave side. He was getting hungry and decided to take a lunch break before trying to move the big one. Piper was happily running around in the woods, but once he started eating, she was there begging. After eating he dragged the cable down to the big rock. He had already dug around the rock and set the cable net, so he just needed to hook up the cable and pray it moved. Mike had warned him not to stand near the cable when he tried moving the big rock. He said cables can break and be dangerous. Raymond knew all about cables breaking. As he backed away the thought of Papa and Kirk's cable accident came to mind, and he paused to think of them and their tragedy. He wondered if they suffered or lay hurt at the bottom of the shaft with no one to help. He was the only person who knew what happened to them and vowed not to stop until he found out the whole truth.

Raymond and Piper stood in the entrance to the little valley. It gave them protection if the cable or tripods broke. When the winch started, he was holding his breath as the cable tightened and the net slid under the rock. The cable slack was gone, and it was beginning to make straining sounds. The cable was tight and making sounds like a guitar string as it got tighter. The tripod near the rock was sinking into the dirt, but the rock still was not moving. Suddenly the dirt in front of the rock started to move, then the rock moved. It was moving slowly but it was moving. The winch had shifted into low gear and the rock was heading towards the incline below the cave. The rock was one hundred feet from the base of the incline, and it took almost two minutes until it reached the base. Raymond was now feeling confident the winch and cable were strong enough to do the job. He and piper stayed in the entrance until the rock reached the top by the cave. Once the rock was at the top, he stopped the winch and walked up the hill to the cave.

The hardest part of winching was over. Now the rock was ready to move down the ravine, and up the other side to the truck fifty feet away, thought Raymond. The rock was not on the truck yet, but he felt relief now that it was close. Raymond and piper stood inside the cave to be safe while the rock made its way down the ravine and up the other side. Once the rock was next to the truck, he and Piper left the cave and headed to the truck. The rock looked insignificant compared to the big truck, but it must have weighed a quarter of its weight. He looked at the rock for a bit before winching it up. Raymond walked towards the front of the truck before winching the rock onto it. Once the rock was on the truck he sat on the ground and relaxed. It had been a long day and more stressful than anything he had felt. He climbed onto the truck and secured all the rocks to it. It was time to head down the dirt road to the house. Hopefully, Mike made sure the brakes were in working order before loaning it out.

The truck moved a bit slower under the weight of all the rocks, but the green beast was heading down the dirt road. The truck cleared the road on the way up and even more on the way down. The logging company would be pleased with the results. Raymond kept the truck in low gear going down the dirt road to be safe. When he reached the gate Raymond unlocked and made sure he relocked it before heading home. He would be coming up again soon and wanted to make sure no one could come through without authorization. He parked the truck behind the barn when he got home. He covered the rocks with a tarp for the trip to Boeing, then went into the house ready for dinner and sleep. Stella met him at the door and asked how things went. Raymond told her loading the rocks was a success and he was taking them for a trip in the morning. She looked at him and asked where the rocks were going. He smiled and said he was going to head to Boeing to talk to people. "Remember you owe me a ride before you give it back to Mike," she said. "I know," he said smiling, "but after my meetings." We do not want to drive that green beast around with such a heavy load. "Once the truck is empty, I will take you up the dirt road to see the little valley and cave," said Raymond.

5

GETTING TO THE BOTTOM

With the rocks safely loaded on the truck Raymond felt a bit of relief. It was time to figure out what really happened to Papa. He knew about Papa's accident and the broken equipment, but not the whole story. The next step would be to find the bottom of the shaft and what happened to Papa and Kirk. They had borrowed two miles of stainless-steel cable and that gave him a starting point for the depth. The accurate depth was particularly important to know. What if Papa had not checked the depth and that caused their accident? Raymond knew finding the depth was imperative to his success and began brainstorming ideas. After a while, the idea of using deep sea Kevlar cable was the perfect solution. It was lite weight, stronger than steel, and he knew a marine research biologist that could help. They do deep sea research dropping cameras down to great depths using Kevlar cable and large drum winches. Next were lights and cameras to see what was at the bottom. Raymond knew his biologist friend was a rockhound nut and might help if he gave him one or more of the smaller rocks still up in the valley. With a good plan it was time for dinner and bed after a long exhausting day.

After breakfast Raymond took Piper for a walk up the dirt road. Stella suggested not walking up the trail to the valley to make sure no one followed and discovered the secrets. The walk up the road was easier than the trail, and Piper would not need to cross the marsh again. After reaching the spot where the rocks had been, he inspected the road and ravine. It was imperative to clear any sign of moving the rocks. The ground in the ravine was soft and covered with fallen leaves and bushes. The cable nets kept the rocks from digging too deeply but there was a visible trail down one side and up the other where the truck stood. It was early fall and soon the leaves would cover the damage, but to be sure, Raymond decided to do a bit of trail covering. He broke a rake sized branch off a bush and walked down into the ravine sweeping the fallen leaves into the depression caused by dragging the rocks. When he finished, it was not perfect, but it would take an experienced tracker to see the trail. It was not hunting season yet, so most likely no one would walk up the dirt road for a month or more. By then the fall leaves would finish covering the trail.

With the trail covered he went down into the little valley to get rocks to convince his friend to loan him one of the deep-sea winches. Luckily, he would be able to borrow the equipment with a camera and lights. Raymond wore a hunting frame backpack to carry the heavy rocks. The rocks were too heavy to carry, one the size of a grapefruit, in his hands all the way back home. He attached a metal box slightly bigger than a coffee can to hold the rocks from moving. Before loading the rocks, he hung the pack from a tree at shoulder height, because it would be easier than trying to pick it up and put it on when loaded. The first rock he chose was a bit bigger than an egg and must have weighed twenty-five pounds, which was twice the weight of a shotput. Next, he tried picking up a rock the size of an orange and could hardly lift it, so he picked one a bit smaller. It must have weighed fifty pounds and was almost impossible to lift onto the pack. The last stone was beautiful with a clear gold tint crystal. *This one should get me a drum winch and camera gear,* he thought. With the two stones finally loaded onto the pack frame it was time to put it on.

Raymond was glad he hung the pack from the tree. It easily weighed eighty pounds and would make carrying through the ravine tough. With Piper playfully running through the woods he made his way down into the ravine and up the other side. He had carried a heavy pack before and knew going slow and easy was the key. Picking your trail was even more important. If he fell, getting up again would be nearly impossible in the soft dirt. He used two long sticks for support and at times needed to use small trees to pull himself up the ravine to the logging road. Once on the road he found a stump to rest the pack on and took a break. The hike down the road was not too bad and after thirty minutes he reached the paved road. The last part was downhill on pavement and went easier. Once home he went to his van and put the pack in the back, so he would not have to pick it up again until he met with his friend.

Raymond went into the house, told his wife what he had done and about the plans for the rocks he brought. She suggested he eat lunch, call his friend, then take a break. Great idea he said, I am tired from packing rocks. While they ate lunch, they talked about the plans for the rocks he packed out this morning. He told her using a deep-sea exploration drum winch with a camera at the end would allow him to reach the bottom and see what was down there. He was careful not to mention the destroyed cable and winch equipment he found. Information like that would come out after he knew for sure what happened to Papa. When they had finished lunch and talked, Raymond called his friend. When he answered, Raymond instantly recognized the voice. "Hi Bonner, how are you doing these days," he asked.

"Holy heck is this Raymond," asked Bonner. "It sure is my old friend, do you have time to get together and talk about a project I need your specific talent for?" "Absolutely," Bonner said. "My crew and I got in five days ago from testing new equipment and I have time this afternoon, if you want to drive into Seattle, because I know how you like trees and dirt," he added. "Well, Mr. Bonner, I cannot believe you're off the water and getting your webbed toes dirty." "I see you are still the funny guy Raymond," Bonner quipped. All right Bonner, I can be there in an hour, and you be ready for a huge surprise, one you could never imagine. Now you have my full attention you old land lover, see you in an hour. If you can stay for dinner my crew caught tuna and are planning a cookout right on the dock tonight. "Count my stomach and I in for that," said Raymond. "See you soon web toes," he added. Raymond told his wife he was heading out right away and would not be home for dinner. She told him if he did not bring that fresh cooked tuna home for her not to come home. All right my hungry lady, tuna for you tonight even if I must wrestle it away from Bonner, and the crew. Stella gave him a hug and told him to hurry home so she could eat like a queen.

The drive to Seattle went by quickly and he was standing on the dock with his pack on in just over an hour. Bonner's exploration ship was easy to spot at the docks. Not because it was twice the size of the other ships, but it looked like a gray whale. Raymond knew Bonner loved the sea and every being in it, but his passion for rare rocks and minerals made him the perfect choice for help. The pack was heavy and walking up the ramp to the ship was more difficult because the ship and ramp moved with the waves. The ship was doing a bit more rocking due to a ferry pulling in. By the time he stepped on the ship Bonner was there to meet him. After a quick greeting Raymond asked if they could go somewhere private. The look on Bonner's face showed his curiosity was peaked, and he turned and went into a door thirty feet from the ramp. Inside Raymond asked him for help taking off the heavy pack.

Bonner snickered and said, "it looks like it was a light frame pack with a small metal box and two small rocks inside, so, are you that old?" asked Bonner.

Raymond turned around and told him to take it off then. As soon as he tried to lift the pack he failed with a grunt and Raymond laughed. "What is in that thing," asked Bonner?

"Just two little rocks," said Raymond. The two men worked together to get the pack off and on to a table. With the pack sitting on the table, it was apparent the small steel box only had two rocks inside. Raymond was smiling as Bonner lifted the egg sized rock and almost dropped it. "Holy mother, what is this thing?" he asked. Just a small rock, web toes, now pick up the bigger one. After two tries, he was able to lift the rock out, and nearly crushed his fingers setting it on the table.

"All right my friend what are these things," Bonner asked?

"To be honest I am not exactly sure, but something like crystal gold but much heavier," Raymond replied.

Bonner was moving and turning the stones best he could with their weight when Raymond asked, "do you like them, and would you consider a trade for them?"

Heck Raymond, I would consider trading the ship if the bank did not own half.

"How about you loan me one of your drum winches with a Kevlar cable and a camera and you can have the stones," said Raymond.

"Is that all you want," asked Bonner? I would give you a whole setup for these stones. And what do you need my equipment so badly for you would trade these incredible stones for?

"I can't tell you everything, but I need it to drop down into an angled shaft to find out what is at the bottom," said Raymond.

"Is it water filled," asked Bonner?

"Not sure," Raymond answered. "We have a new unit that needs testing which will take four months. The unit we are loaning you is brand new innovative technology, and it has interesting features that might be perfect for your needs," Bonner explained.

The unit has five miles of Kevlar cable on the drum, a camera, equipped with radar, sonar, infrared, and this one can operate in the water, and on land using its tank tracks. "To make it even better, it has six arms that can operate a variety of tools," he said. Bonner added, "it can work in underwater caves with both water and land to traverse. It can evaluate air quality, temperature and has a fantastic long-range camera with powerful zoom capabilities. Its primary mission is to inspect and collect samples in the cave systems in South America." Bonner looked at the stones again and asked, "are you sure you want to give these up just for a loan?"

"Yes, because I know you would love to have the stones, and honestly, I have ten more," said Raymond. "Have you had the stones evaluated," asked Bonner? Not yet but I am heading to a lab in a couple of days and will tell you what I find out about them when the results are in. All right Raymond, I will have my guys bring the equipment to your place tomorrow and show you how to operate it. "In the meantime, I will play with my new rocks, assuming I can move them to my lab, said Bonner. "Now it is time for fresh tuna mister rock bringer. "Oh, and can you send a plate home with me for Stella, or I will need to live in the barn," Raymond said. Both men were laughing as they went back on deck to eat.

The next morning a truck pulled into the driveway loaded with the gear he needed. After transferring the winch and rover onto his ATV trailer, the men went through the operating instructions. True to his words the tracked rover was fantastic. It had a handheld wireless remote with a built-in monitor with a twenty-mile range when it was off the cable. The battery powered rover could detach from the cable and drive underwater or on land for hours before needing to reattach for recharging. The winch and rover were light enough to pull with a four-by-four ATV. After saying thanks to Bonner's men Raymond went inside to let Stella know he was heading up to the cave to try out the new toy. She asked if he wanted the lunch she had already packed knowing he could not go more than one minute without trying the equipment out. "You know me well, sweet lady," he said. With Piper trotting alongside he drove up to the cave for the first trial of the equipment.

After unloading the winch, he anchored it to the cave floor and two trees for extra safety. Bonner was not sure if the rover would slide down the steep shaft with its tracks and instructed him to make sure there was no slack in the cable when he began the decent into the shaft. Raymond told Bonner about the smooth surface of the shaft, and how his shoes slid uncontrollably, but his bare feet and Piper's paws did not. One of the crew members had an idea to add leather pads to the rover tracks in hopes natural materials would grip. With a deep breath and a prayer Raymond turned on the remote control and slowly drove it towards the shaft entrance. With a quick check to make sure there was no slack in the cable, Raymond edged the Rover over the edge into the shaft. The Rover had a good grip on the slick surface, so Raymond tried allowing a little slack in the cable to see what happened. The crewman's idea was a success. The tracks with the leather pads did not slide. For an unknown reason natural materials do not slide on the shafts smooth surface. It was now time to try finding the bottom of the shaft and what secrets it held of Papa's disappearance.

Even at top speed the Rover could only reach fifteen miles an hour and he had it going half speed to be safe. That speed allowed him to examine the shaft more closely on the way checking for signs of Papa's accident. Raymond sat on a box to relax and watched the view on his monitor as it descended. He was not sure if Papa had measured the depth of the shaft or not. If he had, then it would take at least twenty minutes. The monitor on the remote control was a large and truly clear camera with the zoom option, and macro lens allowed him to see things the size as a grain of sand in detail. As the rover descended, the monitor showed a continuous view of the same boring smooth surface. Raymond was amazed throughout the rover's descent that there had not been any change in the interior shaft surface. It all looked smooth and clear with no signs that Papa had been through it. The monitor showed the Rover had travelled almost two miles, so Raymond dropped the speed to one-quarter of the speed. Just as the rover hit the two-mile mark Raymond noticed that there was light visible further down the shaft. At first, he thought the light ahead was a reflection off the shaft wall, but as the rover continued down the shaft the light became brighter.

Raymond was on his feet staring at the monitor in disbelief watching the light become brighter as the rover descended. He decided to slow the rover down to a slow walking pace to be careful. The light was now bright enough that he could see the end of the shaft and what looked like a bright room at the bottom. The rover was now close enough to the bottom that he could see something on the floor just on the outside of the shaft. He slowed the rover to a slow crawl to be careful as it came out onto the floor just outside the shaft. What he saw broke his heart. He stopped the rover just outside the shaft to pan the camera over a large amount of wood debris and cable. As he inspected the debris he was prepared for the worst? He wanted to find Papa and Kirk but hoped he would not find signs of bodies. After inspecting the debris from a distance Raymond moved the rover forward and continued around the debris for further inspection. When he finished inspecting the debris field, he had not found any bodies. His relief became wonder. What happened to Papa and Kirk?

With no apparent bodies or bones Raymond was now wondering if they had lived after reaching the bottom. He decided he should start inspecting the area around the debris field to look for signs that they had survived the fall. When he turned the rover around, he could not believe what he was seeing. The rover was in a huge cavern with a large lake going down the center and light coming from somewhere above. Each side of the cavern had terraces that were covered with plants. What he saw was beautiful. How could the cavern have lights and plants so deep under the earth? The cavern was huge, unbelievable, and the light appeared to be coming from a light as bright as the sun, but it was one continuous band in the center of the ceiling that went in both directions as far as he could see. Raymond began using the rover's instruments to check for temperatures and distances.

The rover's instruments showed the temperature was 76 degrees. Raymond was not a geologist, but he knew 76 degrees was highly unusual for underground temperatures. He wondered if the lake was geothermally heated. He checked the distance from where he was standing on one side of the cavern to the other and found that it was over two miles wide. The lake in the center was almost one mile wide and a constant 76 degrees. The distance from the lakeshore to the top of the cavern was a mile. When he tried checking the distance either to the left or to the right of the cavern it was too far to get a reading. Raymond could not believe that an underground cavern this size could exist. Even more unbelievable was the temperature and the fact it had a light source in the center of the ceiling. When he analyzed the light coming from the ceiling it was as full spectrum as the sun. Having a full spectrum of light meant it was able to grow those plants on each side of the cavern. In his wildest imagination, Raymond never thought he would ever see something so incredible as this cavern.

He needed to do more exploration, but it was time to resume searching for Papa and Kirk. He started searching the area nearest the debris field to see if he could find any indication that Papa and Kirk had stayed in the area. He turned the thermal imaging camera on, drove the Rover to the left, and started scanning the area as he drove it forward. After two miles he had seen no indication of human activities of any sort and turned the rover around to go in the other direction. While he was heading back to the debris field position, he scanned the terraced area alongside the lake and began taking pictures and movies to see if he could later have the plants identified. When the rover reached the debris field, he took more pictures to identify and search under magnification. He then drove the Rover another two miles in the other direction, and still found no evidence of any human activity. He was unable to find any sign such as garbage, or a fire that any human had ever been in that area. The thermal imaging camera never found anything that was above the 76-degree ambient temperature of the surrounding area. With the temperature and plants, Raymond expected to see animals in the cavern but found none. He knew he was going to have to find another way to search further in both directions when he came back. He was grateful that the rover had arms that could take samples and decided to go up to the terraced area with the plants.

He drove the rover over to the plants and up the hill toward the first level of the terraced side. He continued to take movies and close-up pictures of the various plants as the Rover climbed. When he reached the first terrace, he found that the flat area was two-hundred feet wide and very level. While the rover was taking pictures, Raymond noticed that the plants were in an orderly fashion. The plants looked like a garden. Each garden was four-hundred feet long, then it repeated over and over for as far as he could see. It was obvious the gardens were not natural. Because of the sheer size he was sure it could not have been Papa and Kirk because they would not have had the time or the energy to have planted gardens this large over such a large area. After inspecting the first terrace, he drove the rover up to the second terrace and found an almost exact duplicate of the first terrace. There were eight more terraces, and he decided to climb to the top to see if they were all identical.

When he reached the top terrace, it also was identical to the other nine terraces. Since they were all the same plants on every terrace, he started taking plant samples to take back up the shaft so that he could have them sampled in a lab to find out what the plants were, and hopefully who planted them. While the rover was on the top terrace, he took more readings of temperature light and scanned the area with a thermal imaging camera once more. He was surprised to find out that the temperature on the top terrace was exactly 76 degrees like the temperature on the first terrace. After scanning the area, he began collecting plant samples. After collecting the samples Raymond drove the rover back down the terraces to where the debris field was. He was disappointed but relieved that he did not find any human remains by the debris field. It was now time to head back up the shaft. He knew since he had not found any indication of human activity or remains that he would need to come back and somehow go further down the cavern in search.

When picking up the rover, Bonner told him he was unsure whether the rover would be able to drive back up the shaft; if not, Raymond would have to use the winch to bring it up. With the plant samples on board, he drove the rover to the shaft and attempted driving up. He was pleased the rover appeared to have no problem driving up the shaft, so he set the winch to automatically reel in the cable as the rover drove up. It took longer driving up than it did going down, but the rover made the trip back to the surface easily. Once it reached the top, he shut the rover off, removed the plant samples, and put them in a cooler. It did not take long to detach the winch cable and load the rover back on to the trailer. On the way down the logging road Raymond had time to think about the cavern and all the fantastic discoveries inside. He began planning for the next visit down the shaft to the cavern but this time he intended to go along with the rover. He knew the rover was not powerful enough to take him down into the cavern and back up so he began planning another way he could access the cavern.

Once home, Raymond parked the trailer carrying the rover, in the barn and went into the house to talk to his wife. Grandma was sitting in her chair by the window as usual and he said hello as he walked by. She gave a nod, said hi, and turned back to look out the window. He wished he could tell her what he found but did not want to upset her. Although he found the wreckage at the bottom of the cavern there was no sign that Papa or Kirk had lived. He decided to wait until he knew for sure what had happened to Papa and Kirk. It was lunchtime and he was hungry so headed into the kitchen. Stella was in the kitchen and looked at him when he came in, so he decided to tell her what he had found so far.

He explained about the cable set up outside the Cave and the debris at the bottom of the shaft. He told her that he suspected Papa and Kirk had fallen down the shaft, but there was no indication that humans had died because there was no sign of bodies, or bones. Before saying anymore, he asked her to follow him into the office and put the rover's memory card into the computer. While the card was loading onto the computer Raymond explained that she would not believe him if he told her what he saw so he had to show her pictures instead. He fast forwarded to the bottom of the shaft, and she watched silently looking over the debris field. He told her he was sure the debris field was from an accident up in the Cave where the cable broke loose and slipped down the shaft into the cavern. He explained there was no sign of human remains in the debris field, but he would have the film analyzed later by an expert. When the rover's camera panned away from the debris field out into the center of the cavern, he could hear Stella take a deep breath, then say, "oh my god."

While they were watching the video, he told her how big the cavern was and that the green she could see was actually plants. As the camera panned up to the top of the cavern, he explained that the light bar she could see was a mile away and went in both directions as far as he could see. He stopped the video and let her know he drove the rover two miles in either direction from the debris field looking for any sign that Papa and Kirk had been there. He told her they survived the fall and they had gone down the cavern looking for a way out. Once the video started, he fast forwarded to where the rover was going uphill to the first terrace. Stella said she could not believe her eyes, how is it plants could grow in a cavern? He told her he had the rover check the temperatures of the air and the water. He also explained that the light coming from the light bar is full spectrum and capable of growing plants just like under a grow light. Raymond told her about taking samples from the plants that were in the area, and how he was going to have them evaluated to see what type of plants they were. While they were watching the video of the rover traveling through the plants Stella noticed that the plants were in a grid that kept repeating itself as far as they could see. "This looks manufactured, is it possible that Papa and Kirk did this," she asked? I do not believe so Stella. The cavern is so huge it would be impossible for just two people to have planted it.

I know it is not natural he said, but I do not believe Papa and Kirk were the ones that planted it. The cavern is so large that I was unable to see the other side and the rover's instruments were unable to detect either end. The cavern is too large for the rover to be able to make it to the end, he said. It will take something faster with a longer range than the rover to be able to explore the cavern further. Looks like I need to think of another method to explore safely, he thought. Because the light source at the top of the camera is full spectrum, I believe it will be possible to use solar panels to charge and run any equipment I need to explore. It may be possible to use an electric ATV for further exploration. I am sure electricity will be much safer and cleaner than gas in that cavern. I would hate to do anything to upset the ecological balance inside, he said. Tomorrow I am going to drive the 8X8 with the rocks on it to Boeing and have their laboratory check it out. While there they might be able to evaluate and identify the plants I collected as well. Stella was shaking her head in disbelief. Raymond, I hope you can find out what happened to Papa. Please do whatever it takes to find answers.

6

GO TO BOEING

Early the next morning Raymond loaded the plants onto the big green 8X8 and headed into the Seattle Boeing plant. He carried the contract that Papa and Bill Boeing had signed and hoped that that would get him into the lab. Driving the big eight-by-eight up the freeway was an experience not everyone would enjoy. The drive was uneventful, and he arrived at the laboratory without incident. He had called the laboratory to make sure it was still in existence and to find out if he could have a meeting with the head of the laboratory. When he called, the operator was not going to connect him to the head of the laboratory until he told her he had an original contract signed by Bill Boeing in 1936 regarding a loan. The head of the laboratory was quite curious when he came to the phone. His first question was what the loan was about. Raymond told him it had something to do with a special rock loaned to Bill Boeing in 1936 in exchange for two miles of steel cable. The laboratory head asked if Raymond would come to the lab as soon as possible, so they could talk in person, not over the phone. He told Raymond his name was David Sinclair and to ask for him when he got to the lab. "I'll be there in two days," Raymond replied.

When he drove the big green eight-by-eight into the laboratory parking lot the guard at the gate was not going to allow him in until Raymond told him to call the laboratory head to verify why he was there. It took less than a minute for the guard to let him in and told him to park the big green eight-by-eight over near the lab's back loading dock. After parking, he carried the cooler with the plants inside around the building into the main entrance. The lady at the front desk looked at him strangely because he was carrying a large cooler and asked if she could help him. When he explained that he had a meeting with David Sinclair she immediately picked up the phone and made a call. Within a couple of minutes, a man walked into the lobby and walked over to Raymond. After the introduction David asked Raymond to follow him. They went through the door and into the laboratory behind. David asked Raymond what was in the cooler. When Raymond explained it contained unusual plants, and needed to be tested, David made a call. Within minutes a dozen people in white coats came into the room. David asked them to take the cooler to the bio lab and run the plants inside through a complete battery of tests. Two lab workers picked up the cooler and left.

David introduced Raymond to the remaining lab workers and suggested they go to the main research lab to talk in private. The main research lab was large and contained instruments and equipment Raymond had never seen before. The group walked to a large table, and everyone sat down. Raymond took the envelope with the contract out of his pocket and handed it to David Sinclair to read. After reading the contract David looked at Raymond, and asked what he knew about the rock, and where they came from. "To be honest I do not exactly know what the rock is, or what it is made of," said Raymond. "I know exactly where they came from," he added. "I do not suppose you would like to tell me where they came from, would you," asked David. "Not yet, I need to talk to you before I let the secret out," said Raymond. "I didn't think so and I really cannot blame you," he replied to David. "How about I tell you what we have learned examining the rock," said David. "That would be great," said Raymond.

Obviously, I was not working here when your relative loaned the rock to Mr. Boeing in 1936. "That makes sense, otherwise you would be retired," said Raymond. David smiled and went on. Since 1936 our lab has been evaluating the rock. To be honest we have been afraid to do too many tests because we knew the rock was on loan. What we do know is this rock is highly unusual and we have seen nothing like it ever before. It is not natural. It is heavier than any element found on earth by over ten times. Over the years we have taken small pieces off the large stone to run tests on. The tests show the clear material is crystallized gold which has an incredibly dense structure. The outer portion is a mixture of waste minerals. Our hypothesis is, extreme heat, and pressure made the crystal. The exterior appears to be a waste byproduct made during the manufacturing process, like slag during steel manufacturing. If allowed to do a more complete destructive testing, we would be able to determine much more than we have, said David. Raymond smiled and said, since I will not be able to bring the cable back, the contract is now void. You can perform any test on the rock you currently possess, because it is now your property.

The look on David's face was priceless as were the faces of the ten people in the white lab coats around the table. David stared at Raymond, and the lab workers started talking amongst one another. If I read your face correctly when you said, "currently possess," you were leading up to something," said David. I can say without a doubt it is going to be a big and heavy surprise, said Raymond. The talk around the table stopped, and now everyone was staring at Raymond.

"I want to do exploration and need money to purchase and manu-facture the equipment needed," said Raymond. I brought along items I would like to sell to fund my exploration. "By chance is there anyone in this room that has experience driving an army eight-by-eight with a crane," asked Raymond? Two of the lab workers raised their hands. With David's permission, please go to the back of the building by the loading dock and drive the green eight-by-eight inside. I am sure you would like to keep what is on that truck secret, so it would be best to bring it inside," said Raymond. He handed the truck keys to one of the lab workers, and they went to bring the truck inside.

"I assume I am going to need to call someone in corporate immediately am I right," asked David.

Raymond looked at him and nodded, then said "I believe you will need someone high up in corporate with the ability to plan on this matter.

Without another word David stood up, said please excuse me I will be right back, and left. The remaining lab workers sat with Raymond and waited for him to return. "What kind of work do you do in this lab," asked Raymond.

One of the workers spoke up, and said this lab is to study the rock about which we have been talking. A whole lab for that one rock you received in 1936, asked Raymond. "The importance of that rock to science your relative loaned us goes way beyond its value in gold," replied the worker.

"I am not a scientist, so there is no way I can understand how one rock would be worth funding a laboratory of this size and quality," said Raymond. The rock is unlike any rock we have seen or evaluated. "Aside from its incredible weight and density, the rock has properties we have never seen before or even imagined," he said. Raymond was trying to wrap his head around what the lab worker said when David walked into the room with three new people.

David introduced the three people to Raymond and explained they were the president, vice president, and CEO of Boeing. If he needed a decision today, they were the ones who could make it. The two lab workers that went to bring in the eight-by-eight walked into the room while David spoke to the Boeing people. Raymond suggested that everyone go down into the lab to see what was on the truck. When they got to the truck Raymond asked if someone would remove the tarps to show what was under them. After the rocks were revealed, no one spoke. Everyone was staring at the back of the truck in disbelief. David looked at Raymond and asked, "are those rocks what I think they are?"

Raymond nodded, and said, "yes, they are."

David looked at the three Boeing execs then climbed onto the back of the truck to inspect the rocks. After five minutes inspecting the rocks, he said "are you serious Raymond? Do you have any idea the value of even the smallest rock on this truck," he asked?"

"To be honest, I don't have a clue. I assumed they were worth the weight of the gold in them," said Raymond.

David climbed down from the truck, walked to the three Boeing executives and asked them to come with him. They walked across to the other side of the loading area and talked. When they had finished talking, the three executives came over to Raymond. The CEO said, "name your price, and it is yours, and David Sinclair will help draw up the paperwork." They all said thank you, shook hands and left. David came over to Raymond and said, "they meant what they said Raymond, name your price." "I sincerely do not get it,"said Raymond. "Let me be honest with you,"said David. I can tell you have no concept of the value these rocks have to science, and what it means to the Boeing companies future. It is near impossible to put a dollar value of these rocks to science and how it could advance human technology hundreds of years. The properties of these rocks that we have already discovered and will discover in the future are unimaginable. The new scientific knowledge gained will allow Boeing to outpace every other company in the world. That knowledge means big money in the corporate world. By big money I mean an amount with more than two zeros after it. They were being honest; you can name your price.

Raymond was speechless, just staring at David not knowing what to say or do. They thought you might be out of your league with this type of money. They have instructed me to tell you what the real value is in terms of money. Let us go back to the table and sit down, because you are really going to need it. When seated, David started by telling Raymond the average cost of a Boeing 747 is over four hundred million dollars. The rocks you brought today are worth at least ten times the amount of a 747 to the Boeing Corporation. I understand that figures this high are startling to you. The Boeing company wants to be honest and fair because of the impact these rocks will have on its future. They have offered to give you a fair price and set up a corporate entity in your name to professionally manage it. They have also offered you the assistance of their chief financial officer to help you. I am serious Raymond; we are talking about four billion dollars offered to you for those rocks on the truck. From the look on your face, I can tell you are going to need that chief financial officer. His responsibility is to help you better understand the money and protect you from somehow losing it. Please understand Raymond, the value may be much higher to the Boeing company's future than four billion dollars. That is why their offer is so generous. They also hope you will share information about your secret place where the rocks came from. It is of great scientific importance we could study how these rocks formed.

"You are right David, I totally cannot comprehend $400 million let alone $4 billion,"said Raymond. By the time we leave this room, the chief financial officer will have set up a bank account with four hundred million for your immediate use. Then he will set up a payment schedule to pay off the rest of the four billion over the next few years. "Did you say a bank account with four hundred million in a bank today," asked Raymond? Yes, four hundred million today, if you agree to sell the rocks. "I would like to offer you a ride home while they unload the truck, they will deliver the truck to your home," said David. "I am honestly not sure if I am going to throw up or pass out," said Raymond. "I can imagine this is an immense shock and will take a while for you to get back to normal," said David. Not that you can ever be normal again with that kind of money.

"Did you say, they are going to give me four hundred million when I leave today?" asked Raymond.

"Yes, they really are," said David. "I am glad you had me sit for this because I am sure I would be on the floor right now," said Raymond. My God, how am I going to tell my wife that this is real? Well, for one I imagine the chief financial officer is going to give you paperwork that should be of help in convincing her. David's phone rang, and after two minutes' talking, he said it was time to go and meet with the chief financial officer.

David led Raymond out of the lab into an office where a man in a suit was sitting. The man stood immediately, and walked over to Raymond, and introduced himself as Stephen Bell, CFO of the Boeing Co. After the introduction David told Raymond that it was time for him to go. Now he had new rocks that needed to study and said goodbye. Raymond watched him walk away and turned back to Stephen Bell. Raymond was standing silently staring at Stephen in disbelief of what had just transpired over the last two hours. Stephen saw the look in his eyes and suggested they have a seat and talk. I understand what you must be going through Raymond. I work with large sums of money every day, and I am having a tough time believing the amount of money they offered you for your find. I am not a scientist, so it is hard for me also to understand why the company is offering such a huge sum of money for a bunch of rocks. Obviously, the rocks you have brought in must be of immense value to the company. In all my years as a CFO, I have never seen such a large financial transaction offered to a private citizen. That said, I want you to know that I am at your disposal anytime you need help through this transition, and in the future. First, we have important paperwork to take care of. Afterwards we will drive you home. Today you ride home in style and really impress your wife. It may be easier for her to believe you since the CEO has loaned us his limousine and driver to take you home. I will also be going along to help explain to your wife the situation, plus it will give us extra time on the drive for me to talk to you about the money, and how I can help.

The ride home in the limousine was comfortable, but Raymond was in such shock he did not remember much of it. He had a tough time understanding what Stephen was talking about because the numbers were so large. When they arrived at the house, they went inside to meet his wife and talk to her about their new financial situation. Raymond introduced Stella to Stephen and suggested they go into the office to talk. Raymond told Stella about going to Boeing and their reactions to the new rocks. When he got to the part about the three top corporate officers meeting with him, and the offer, she had a look of disbelief on her face. Stephen told Stella he understood that this was difficult to believe. He assured her the money the company offered was real and handed her financial papers that showed that they now had four hundred million in the bank. He went on to explain the remaining balance will be in the bank in the next few years. Raymond was beginning to feel a little more comfortable with these large numbers and suggested that Stella could now afford any car she wanted. At that Stella smiled a nervous smile. It is time for me to leave and give you two a chance to talk, said Stephen. It may take two or three days for all of this to fully sink in. "Remember, you have my phone number, and if you need anything, you can call 24 hours a day," said Stephen. Stella stayed in the library while Raymond walked Stephen out to the limousine to say goodbye. When he went back into the office, Stella was still sitting, staring silently in disbelief.

Stella looked at Raymond and asked, is this a dream? No, it is not a dream, and I am having a tough time believing it myself. The money they have given us for rocks is beyond my comprehension, he said. When I drove the truck into Seattle, I had no idea what the rocks were worth. In my wildest dreams, I was hoping for one or two hundred thousand dollars. I could not have imagined anything close to a million, let alone four billion dollars. Truthfully, I was hoping for enough to buy the property around the cave and buy the equipment for more exploration. Not only do we have enough money to buy the property and equipment I need for exploration, but our financial future is now secure. Stella was still holding the financial paperwork and looked at it again while Raymond was talking. "I still can't believe we have four hundred million in the bank," she said. I do not know about you Raymond but all I want to do right now is go outside and scream to the wind. "I know how you feel," he said. "I need to start planning for the next trip down into the cavern, but I think for the next few days we need to stay home and relax, so this can all sink in," said Raymond. Let me tell you one thing Raymond. I do not feel like cooking dinner tonight. I am going to call to get it delivered, said Stella. For the first time today, Raymond was able to laugh. He agreed that having dinner delivered sounded nice, and it is not like we can't afford it now, he said. Raymond sat with Stella for a while trying to calm down and think about what he needed to do next.

The next morning Mike's big green eight-by-eight arrived. Raymond had them leave it in front of the barn because he was taking it back to Mike. The two workers thanked Raymond for letting them drive the green beast. They said they had not had so much fun since they were in the army, and this time, they got to keep their long hair. They told him they were available any time he needed help, especially if they were going to go to where the rocks were. Raymond smiled, and said, when the time comes, he would be glad to have their help and show them where he found the rocks. After saying goodbye, they got into the car that had followed them and headed out. He called Mike to see if he were home so that he could bring the eight-by-eight back. Mike answered and said he would be there for a while, so Raymond decided to head over and bring the truck back. On the way over to Mike's he thought about what he could tell Mike about what he was doing, because Mike was going to be invaluable in building and designing the things he would need for further exploration of the cavern.

7

NEW MONEY AND NEW TOYS FOR EXPLORING

S tella and he decided not to tell anyone about the windfall of money until they had a lawyer to help figure everything out. After parking the truck, Raymond asked Mike to sit down to go over things that he had been thinking about, and ideas that he needed help with. Raymond produced a story that he needed an electric 4X4 ATV that can go long distances and carry solar panels to recharge on the trip. When Mike asked him where he was going, he said, planning on a desert trip to search for rocks. "Sounds hot," replied Mike. That is why I want the solar panels, so I can bring a rechargeable cooler and a couple of fans. Sounds like you will need to be pulling a trailer with extra batteries. "It should be big enough to carry the solar panels, a cooler, and your fans," said Mike. Any chance you can make the ATV strong enough to pull a trailer big enough I can sleep in? It would be nice sometimes to get out of the sun, and protection from dangerous animals. "How fast do you want it to go and how far without recharging," asked Mike? It would be nice if it could do at least fifty miles an hour at top speed and a range of two hundred miles before recharging. "Well, you will need a trailer with extra batteries to get that kind of range," said Mike. "I have just the motor to get you the power and speed you are looking for," he added. One thing about this setup, Raymond, it is not going to be cheap. Not a problem Mike I have extra cash from selling a fancy rock I found so it should not be a problem. How soon do you think you can have this all put together Mike? "Can you give me a week Raymond," he asked? I happen to have the parts here; it will just take three or four days to put them all together. Perfect Mike, it will take me a week to finish preparing for the trip.

"Thanks Mike," said Raymond, 'see you in a week."

Raymond needed a trailer for the ATV to carry the rover. The electronic instruments it had were to survey the cavern completely. The rover could recharge with its built-in solar panels. Over the next week he gathered the equipment, clothes, and food required for two weeks. He did not expect to need too many clothes because of the temperature in the cavern, and he could wash any dirty ones in the lake. He chose freeze-dried meals to eat because they were lighter, and only needed water to fix them. Water would not be a problem because of the lake, although he had not received the report on the plants and water yet. If the water was bad at least he could bring a filter to make it drinkable. He was going to bring a sun stove to heat his water for his meals and hoped that the light source on the ceiling would be strong enough to make the stove work, otherwise he would be eating cold meals. After only five days, Mike said the ATV was ready. Raymond needed a couple more days to prepare, so he told Mike he would pick it up in a week.

David Sinclair called Raymond the next morning and asked him to come to the lab and talk about the plant samples he had brought in for testing. "Anything wrong," asked Raymond? Not wrong but you should come down so we can talk about them in private.

"Not a problem," answered Raymond. "I can be there in a couple of hours.

"Thanks," said David, I will see you then."

Once he arrived, David met Raymond in the reception room and asked him to follow him to another lab building where they do biological testing. On the way David asked if these plants just happened to come from the same place as the rock samples. "Not the same place, but you could say close," answered Raymond. The lab that David took him into was quite different from the first. This lab had much smaller equipment and was set up for chemical testing rather than mechanical testing. When they got into the new lab David took him over to a small group of people standing around a table looking at a computer monitor.

After introductions, David informed the group that the location where these plants were was near where the rocks were. David asked one of the men to tell Raymond what they had learned about the plants. "Hello Raymond, my name is Larry, and I am the lead of this lab. First, I must tell you every one of these plants is a new species and is unique from anything we have seen before. Our testing shows that all these plants are hybrids. What is most interesting is they were hybrids one hundred thousand years ago. It is almost impossible to determine exactly how long ago they were hybrids. We estimate they were hybrid while humans were still hunter gathers before they had developed any sort of farming. My curiosity as to where you found these and who created them is killing me," said Larry. "I don't suppose I could talk you into telling me where you found these fantastic plants," he added. "Sorry Larry, I am not ready to disclose where I have found the plants or rocks yet," said Raymond. I promise to tell you everything after I have finished my project." "I understand," said Larry, "then let us get to the findings on these plant and water samples."

First the water sample. The water assessed out free of any contamination. It could not be any purer if it had come from a deep underground spring. If this were city water, there would be no need for treatment prior to human consumption. The plant samples are amazing. Like I said before, every one of these plants is a hybrid, every plant has different properties and different nutritional values. The easiest way to put it, is these plant specimens are perfect for human survival. Various plants have elevated levels of good oils. Others have protein levels higher than meat. So high in protein you would not need to eat meat, and they include all the essential amino acids. Three of the plants contain elevated levels of vitamins. If a human were to eat these plants, they would receive all the nutrients their body needs. Absolutely the oddest part is that these plants have flavors you would never get bored eating. After testing to see if they were poisonous, we tasted samples, and they were delicious. "Now are you sure you would not like to tell us where you found these plants," asked Larry. I am sorry Larry; I just cannot divulge any information yet. "Please give me four more weeks to complete my project," said Raymond. "If that is the best you can do Raymond, I will have to wait," said Larry. Thank you for letting us evaluate these samples. David and Larry said goodbye and walked out into the reception room. "Well Raymond, it looks like you are going to hold onto your secrets a little longer," said David. Raymond, hopefully, in four weeks you will get back to us, and share those secrets. "As soon as I can tell you I will," said Raymond. "All right, looking forward to hearing from you in four weeks, until then take care Raymond," said David.

After leaving the lab he headed north to Everett. He found a company by Paine Field that designed a large drone capable of extended flights. It was perfect for exploring the cavern. The drone had been used for military surveillance and is large and capable of charging in flight due to on-board solar charging, and a twin battery system. The drone flies on one battery while the other charges. Its cameras can zoom for closeup pictures and has telephoto capability for up to ten miles. The remote control has a range of fifty miles. If it loses contact it will autonomously return to the starting point or reconnect with the remote signal once it is close enough. The drone is much faster for exploring than the ATV. The drone has a top speed of two hundred miles per hour. The ATV tops out at fifty miles per hour. Pulling the trailer, while gathering data, Raymond planned to keep the speed to around twenty miles per hour. When he first spoke to the owner of the company, he was not going to allow Raymond to use the drone, let alone see it until he offered to donate five million dollars. The owner was more than happy to offer complete access, and use of the drone for that amount of money.

When he arrived at the company, he was surprised how small and unassuming the building was. He went inside, told the receptionist who he was and why he was there and she made a quick call. Within a couple of minutes, a man came out and introduced himself as Tony Baker. Tony took him into the main factory area and showed him around. There were about a dozen workers in the shop, and he could see quite a few of the large drones in various stages of work. While they were touring the shop Tony explained the features of the drones and their expected use in the military. He said he was thankful for the donation and was curious how he intended to use it. Raymond explained he was a geologist and wanted to search every remote and hard to reach location. Tony smiled and said, "those must be special rocks for you to be willing to donate five million dollars to hunt them." "They are special rocks, but honestly, I am more of a hobby geologist and rock collector," said Raymond. I also love high-tech gadgets. My investments have recently given me a good sum of money, so I decided to retire, and start playing more. After reading about your drone development, I knew it was perfect, both for fun and exploring. "Glad to hear about your return on the investments, and grateful for your donation," said Tony. Your donation is a needed windfall for my company. It will allow us to develop more features for the drones, which will bring greater sales.

Tony asked Raymond to step outside and watch a demonstration of one of the drones in action. After watching the drone fly through its paces, he trained on it. The drone was so fast it was hard to watch without the monitor. When the training was complete, they went inside, and Tony surprised him with a catered lunch. During lunch, Raymond met the lab workers who expressed their gratitude for his financial help. They were happy that now there was enough research money to develop ideas that could put the company at the top, and ensure they had jobs for a while. Raymond only planned to borrow the drone, but Tony said the drone was his to keep. He was grateful for the donation, and it would be great to see the drones used for something other than military use. After lunch they assembled all the equipment for the drone and loaded it into Raymond's van. When fully assembled, the drone was almost eight feet across and ten feet long. Even disassembled the drone barely fit in his van. It was a good thing he had Mike build a trailer long enough he could sleep in because he was going to need all that room to fit the drone on top. The drone was light, but it was large. It was a good thing the water in the cavern was clean enough to drink because he was starting to run out of room on the trailer.

On the way home Raymond stopped by Mike's house to pick up the ATV and trailer. When he arrived, he saw, as always, Mike was outside working on a piece of machinery. Mike told him the ATV ran great and had lots of power with the new electric motor. The only question Mike asked was why Raymond wanted leather pads on the tires. Luckily, Raymond had thought about this question and had produced a relevant story. He explained that the ATV might be driving in sensitive areas on sandstone and did not want to cause damage. "Totally understand," said Mike, which is a clever idea. The ATV and its trailer were sitting on a flatbed trailer for hauling home. As Mike was hooking the trailer to Raymond's van, he noticed the drone inside. Raymond could tell by Mike's reaction that he was going to have to explain the drone to him. He told Mike the ATV was perfect for exploring, rock hunting and sleeping in, but wanted something faster. Mike begged him to pull it out so he could look at it. Raymond was not in a hurry and knew Mike would not give up, so they pulled the drone out and assembled it. He was not sure what was keeping Mike from drooling as he was inspecting the drone. Once Raymond assembled it, he flew it around the property for a while to give Mike the full show. After showing him everything the drone could do Raymond decided to really shock Mike. He flew the drone up to two thousand feet altitude, then hit full speed flying back and forth over Mike's house. As expected, Mike was astonished. Mike was still talking a mile a minute after the drone landed while Raymond took it apart, and loaded it back into the van. He had to promise to let Mike play with it when he got back from the trip.

Raymond now had everything he needed to explore the cavern. Once home, he went inside to talk to Stella about the plans for exploring the cavern. She was not happy the plan included his being down there for two weeks, but understood how important it was, and he might return sooner. He told her there would be a powerful transmitter in the cave and the bottom of the shaft. That would enable him to call her, or she could call him whenever needed. She felt relieved, and it also gave him a safety net in the event something went wrong. It took a couple of days to set up the transmitter and load the trailer. Since he was not sure if the ATV would be able to make it up and down the steep shaft into the crater, he decided to use the winch from the rover as a safety line. Once the winch was set up, Raymond went home and said his goodbyes to Stella. It was almost 7 AM and he wanted to get an early start, so it was time to say goodbye. To her credit she did not cry when he hugged and kissed her goodbye. The drive up the dirt road was quiet, which gave him time to relax before the big trip down the shaft. He drove the ATV with the trailer in tow into the cave and hooked it up to the winch cable. With everything secured, and ready to go, he went outside the Cave to make sure nothing was visible. He walked down into the ravine and up the other side making sure to cover up any signs he had driven through there. He was going to be gone for up to two weeks and did not want anybody to find the cave and the winch inside. When he was satisfied no one could find the cave he headed back inside. First, he double checked to make sure the winch cable was secure, then prepared to head down the shaft into the cavern for the first time.

8

THE CAVERN EXPLORATION

The winch had multiple gears to use as a brake to slow decent. Raymond shifted it into a low gear which would keep the ATV from going down too fast and going out of control. He decided to be cautious, and not take a chance, so he set it for walking speed. At that speed it would take about 30 minutes to reach the bottom, but it was much safer. He was a little nervous as the ATV started down the shaft, but right away realized the leather on the tires gave good traction. Since the ATV had good traction, he was able to use its lower gears also. Using the low gear took stress off the winch and less chance of it failing. Now he was certain he would be able to drive the ATV up and down the shaft but decided to continue using the winch as a safety. He did not want to end up at the bottom of the shaft, like Papa's cable and the debris. The ATV lights lit up the shaft and it was beautiful going down. The crystal interior reflected the light and gave it a gold tint which seemed dreamlike as he was traveling down. As the ATV approached the bottom of the shaft, light became visible coming from the cavern, but it did not seem as bright as it did when the rover was down. As he drove out of the shaft into the cavern his first impression was correct. It was darker inside the cavern than before. He drove the ATV inside the cavern beyond the debris pile and stopped. He unhooked the winch cable and secured it to the cable in the debris field. No sense taking any chances, he thought. If someone did find the winch in the cave, at least they would have a tough time winching the cable up. For added security he shut the winch off with the remote and locked it.

Raymond drove towards the lake shore then turned the ATV off. He sat on the ATV staring out at the lake and glancing around the cavern. In this low light he would have a challenging time seeing detail. If he took out the rover, it would be capable of seeing in this low light with its instruments. He had been in the cavern for about 15 minutes trying to decide what to do, when he started to think it might be getting lighter. It was hard to tell for sure, so he sat for just a little longer to see if it did. While waiting, he walked to the lake shore and ate his lunch early. He ate a big breakfast, but after the stressful ride down he felt hungry. While he was eating, he thought about trying plants that were growing on the terraces. The guys at the lab said that the plants tasted good and thought since all he had was freeze dried food, it might be a good option. The lake was very still and there did not appear to be any wind inside the cavern. The temperature was quite comfortable and while he was sitting, he removed his coat and shoes and relaxed. The water was about two feet below the top of the shoreline, so he decided to touch the water with his bare feet. The water felt cooler than the air even though the instruments measured them being the same temperature as the rover's instruments. After another thirty minutes sitting by the shoreline, it was almost full light. He could now easily see the other side of the lake and further down the cavern. He began to wonder if the light in the cavern mimicking night and day cycles of above ground was on a 12/12 hour cycle or not. Whoever made this cavern must have understood plants needed night and day to grow properly. Raymond put his shoes back on and walked over to the ATV.

It was now 8:30 AM, he had been in the cavern an hour, and it was as light as it had been when the rover was down. With full light, it was time to head down the cavern and search for Papa. Before Raymond left, he called Stella to make sure the transmitter was working and to let her know he had made it down safely. She answered immediately and by the sound of her voice he knew she had been nervous. When he explained it had been dark when he got to the cavern, and now it was light she asked him if he was sure he really wanted to go explore. He explained that he thought whoever built this cavern must have incorporated a day and night cycle to make sure the plants would thrive. Also, anyone living inside the cavern would be more comfortable. He promised to be sure there was enough battery power to make it back to the shaft entrance if there was a problem with the light. He told her Mike said the ATV had enough battery charge to go two-hundred miles. He would make sure not to go beyond one-hundred miles. That way he could be sure to make it back if he could not solar charge the batteries. After promising Stella he would call every morning, every night, and at lunch time, so she could be sure he was ok, they said goodbye.

Raymond climbed on the ATV and headed down the cavern along the lake shore. He was not sure which way to go because the cavern appeared endless in either direction. Since he did not know which way he should go, he chose to go to the right. At twenty-miles an hour it would take five hours for the Rover to reach the one-hundred-mile mark, which was the safety point in the event the light in the cavern did not come back on. He was sure the lights would come back on, then go off for a night cycle, but wanted to make sure just in case. He did a quick walk around to make sure everything on the trailer was secure, double checked all the tires, and Raymond was ready to go. After an hour of riding, Raymond noticed plants growing on the terraced sides looked a little different. He drove over to the bottom of the first terrace and parked the ATV. For fear of damaging plants, he chose to walk up and investigate. He could not be sure, but he thought the plants were different. One plant was a light green color, and one plant looked taller. He did not want to waste time looking at the plants, so headed back down to get on the ATV. There would be time on the way back to collect plant samples for testing. Before he left, Raymond took pictures of plants on the terrace for future reference, and comparison.

After two more hours of riding, Raymond again noticed the plants on the terrace appeared to be different. He decided not to walk up this time but took pictures for additional comparison. He had been riding for three hours and traveled approximately sixty miles with no sign Papa had been there. Except for a difference in the plants nothing changed over the sixty miles. Every mile was a carbon copy of the previous mile. Had it not been inside of such an incredible cavern, the scenery would have been as boring as a freeway drive. Raymond planned to ride for another two hours, then stop once he reached the one-hundred-mile mark. After five hours of riding, Raymond was getting tired and stopped for the day. After shutting off the ATV he looked around. This time he was sure the plants up on the terrace were different than ones down the cavern. They looked much taller, and the colors were brighter. He walked up the hill to the first terrace to look at the plants. These plants were different, he thought. They were obviously taller, and the color he noticed was from berries on the plants. The lab tests showed the plants were edible and tasty, so he took a chance and ate one of the berries. He was not sorry he did because it was wonderful. Extremely sweet and juicy. Better than any berry he had tasted. He did not eat any more just to be safe and returned to the ATV.

Raymond stopped the ATV at the base of the hill below the terraces. He had not seen any sign of flooding from the lake but did not want to take any chances. For a while, the thought of sleeping up on the first terrace just to be sure sounded good but decided it was safer inside the trailer. Although he had not seen any signs of life inside the cavern, he felt caution was the best course of action at this time. Before he could prepare the trailer for sleeping, he had to unload the large drone. Since the drone needed to be assembled, he decided to prepare it for its first flight after unloading the trailer. With the drone unloaded it only took five minutes to get the sleeping area ready for the night. There was no way to tell when the light would go out, and he wanted to be able to climb into bed without effort. Once the sleeping area was ready, he set up the solar stove to boil water for his lunch. The light coming from the top of the cavern did not feel hot, but it was warm, and he hoped it would be capable of boiling his water in the solar stove. He had decided not to bring a gas stove for fear of hurting or contaminating the environment inside the cavern. If his solar stove did not work, he would be stuck eating cold food for the two weeks he was in the cavern. If the lab tests were correct, he could also try eating plants along the way, especially the new berries and fruit he had found. He would have to be careful eating the plants in this part of the cavern. The lab had not assessed them yet. To be safe he should only eat one or two berries he found during a twenty-four-hour period. With the solar stove set up to boil water, he began assembling the drone for its first flight in the cavern.

The drone easily went together, and within two minutes Raymond was ready for his first flight inside the cavern. Tony said the drone was waterproof and would float in the event it landed in the water. Since he did not have a way to retrieve the drone if it landed in the lake, he planned to stay over land while he flew it. He knew when on the next visit to the cavern, he would be sure to bring a boat. He could easily carry a rubber raft with an electric motor in the trailer on the next trip. He wanted to check out the other side of the cavern, and a boat would be the only way to safely do it. That is, unless he could find a way across somewhere down the cavern. He started the drone, went through the safety checklist, then flew to an altitude of four-hundred feet, and hovered while he checked the controls and monitor. When he was confident the drone was in good working order, and had full control, he flew it down the cavern. For the first flight he kept the speed down to one hundred mph. At that speed he could only travel thirty minutes before the drone would lose contact with the transmitter. The slower speed allowed him to better observe the inside of the cavern while the drone flew. The cameras would be able to record everything even at top speed, but he decided to keep it slow so he could better personally observe. After twenty-five minutes of flying, he had not seen anything unusual or any site that humans had been there. The drone had flown more than forty-miles, which meant it was nearing its fifty-mile maximum range. He turned the drone around and set it on automatic return and went over to the solar stove to fix lunch.

When Raymond checked the stove, he was pleased to find the water had reached a boiling temperature under the artificial light. The artificial light was indeed good enough to boil water, which ensured him warm meals throughout the expedition. He sat down to relax while eating and waiting for the drone to return. After eating lunch, he walked up to the first terrace level and looked at the plants once more. He picked a couple more of the berries and tasted them. He was careful not to eat more than a couple even though he was confident they were safe after the lab tests. These berries were just as delicious as the ones he tried earlier, and he thought how nice they would be as treats while searching. The drone was approaching, so Raymond went down to inspect it after it landed. The drone looked to be in perfect shape. After shutting it off, he set the computer to data download and sent it to his computer at home. In the event anything happened to him, Stella and he decided that every night he would send the information the drone gathered to their home computer, so she would know what happened. The drone's program would send its information if something happened, like a crash. Once the drone landed, he walked to the lake to relax.

Raymond was not sure what the light cycle was in the cavern, so he decided to sit by the lake shore and relax for a while. He had been in the cavern almost eight hours, with seven of it being light. He had been sitting up relaxing when something caught his eye moving underwater. He could not be sure if he had seen something, because all he saw was a large dark shadow moving incredibly fast. He could swear he saw something, but he had only seen it out of the corner of his eye. He looked towards the top of the cavern in case it was a shadow from something above. He saw nothing above him and continued to look in the water. To be honest, seeing it made him nervous being alone in the cavern. He wondered if there was something alive in there, stood up, and backed away from the lake shore. He was grateful that he parked the ATV and trailer at the base of the hill. It was far enough away from the lake shore so he was sure nothing could jump out and grab him. While he was traveling tomorrow, he would make sure he had the drone keep at least one camera pointed into the lake. He was glad he had Mike build a trailer big enough he could sleep in. Originally, he wanted to sleep in it for fear of something on land. Now he was grateful because of what might be in the lake. After the scare from the lake, he wished he had brought a weapon of some kind, not that he owned one, or that it would have worked under the water.

It was 3 PM, and he assumed there was five hours daylight left, so he went to explore the terraces on foot. Before leaving he grabbed his smart glasses. Tony had included a pair of smart glasses that he could wear while driving the ATV, so that he would not need to watch the monitor when the drone was flying. The smart glasses could take pictures, and films in high definition, as well as access the computer if he needed to look something up or do research. They were also capable of sending data to the drone's computer for storage. He could also use them to call Stella and talk to her any time within two miles of the ATV. He put on the glasses and headed up the hill to inspect the terraces. For fun he called his wife so she could see what the interior of the cavern looked like. After the little scare by the lake, it would be nice to talk to her to help him feel a little more secure. It was better not to tell her he had seen something in the lake until he knew for sure if there was something in there or not. Stella was happy he called and was excited about seeing the interior of the cavern for the first time. He walked up the hill and stopped on the first terrace looking in every direction, so she could see everything. She was amazed at how beautiful but also how big the cavern was. He continued walking upward, stopping at each terrace to pan the surroundings. Stella was enjoying the view, and it was smart to get everything filmed along the way. By the time he reached the 10th and last terrace, he was beginning to feel tired. Riding five hours on an ATV is fatiguing even if the terrain was flat. He walked to the wall of the cavern on the tenth terrace to get a closer look at it.

The cavern wall was identical to the wall inside the shaft. Like the shaft wall, it also was crystal with a gold tint. He was glad he made the deal with Boeing earlier, otherwise after seeing this much of the crystal rock, they might not have paid him quite that much. He already had four hundred million in the bank account, so if Boeing decided not to pay him the rest of the $4 billion, he would not be too upset. Stella had been quiet while he walked up the hill, and across each terrace, but when he got to the cavern wall, she commented on how beautiful it was. She asked him jokingly if they could build a lake place on the top terrace. "The backdrop of that crystal wall, and the view of the lake would make a wonderful place to live," she said. Raymond told her that the temperature was still 76 degrees at the top, and honestly would have been perfect for a lakeside vacation retreat. While he was walking and scanning the area, Stella said she noticed something odd. She had moved into the library and was watching Raymond exploring on the computer monitor. "The larger screen of the monitor enabled her to see things Raymond could not see with his eyes, or smart glasses," she said. "What do you mean," asked Raymond? It looks like there are grooves or depressions on the floor of the terraces. "Are you sure," he asked? "Quite sure," she said. She suggested he kneel and look down at the terrace floor to see what he could see.

He did what she suggested and sure enough there appeared to be a groove in the floor. He stood up and walked over to the groove and felt it with his hands. She was right, he said. The floor had a slight depression which was a foot wide, one inch deep. He continued walking down the terrace and Stella said it appeared that each time the gardens shifted from one square to another there was a groove. Raymond walked across the terrace floor, across half a dozen square gardens, and sure enough between each garden was an identical depression. He was wondering if the depression was to mark the boundary of each of the gardens. When he told Stella what he thought, she suggested it could also be for irrigation, or water runoff. He agreed and wondered why there needed to be water runoff or irrigation. With all the other wonderful things in the cavern, what if it rained occasionally, she asked? I had not thought about the possibility of it raining inside the cavern, he said. How else would the plants get watered, she asked? That was an amazing find Stella, thank you, said Raymond. It is a good thing I brought a coat, he said. If it rains, I might need it. "One more thing," she said,"can you walk over to the wall and look at it closely please,"she asked? He walked over the wall, stood within a couple of feet of it and asked, what is next.

Please walk slowly to your left while keeping your eyes on the cavern wall, she asked. He did what she asked, and after about fifteen feet walking sideways, she said stop please. That is it, I thought I saw something, she said. What do you see, asked Raymond? I do not see a thing just a crystal wall with a gold tint. Look closer, she said. Try moving one foot to your left, then look at an angle, and see what you can see, she suggested. When he did, he saw what she was talking about. It was a dark line in the otherwise clear wall. He followed the line upwards and about twelve feet from the floor, it curved, then came straight down to the floor. Now that he could see it, Raymond backed up to get a better view. It looks like the shape of an exceptionally large door, said Stella. It really does, he said. The lines are about eight feet wide, twelve feet high, in the shape of a door, but the surface is smooth without a hint of a crack, he added. Do me a favor, continue walking down the wall, to see if there are any more lines like that one, she asked. Sure, enough they found more of the lines in the wall. Each of the gardens was approximately four-hundred feet wide and every one of the garden walls had two door shaped lines in them.

"I do not really know what these lines mean," said Raymond. What I do know is, we have more mysteries than answers on our hands. If those are not doors, do you have any idea what they are, asked Stella? The only thing I can think of is, they are meant for decorations, said Raymond. That is as good a guess as any, she said. After walking all over the terrace checking the floor and the walls, he was feeling hungry and checked his watch. It was past five, and Raymond told her it was time for dinner, then promised to call her at bedtime. Thanks for the tour honey, talk to you later, she replied. Remember not to eat more of those delicious berries, she said and hung up.

After she hung up Raymond smiled and walked down to the

ATV to fix dinner. As he was walking down, he thought of all the secrets this cavern was holding. Where were Papa and Kirk, and what happened to them? Did he really see something in the water, and if he did, what was it? Why was everything in this cavern perfect for humans to live in? The biggest secret of all, he thought, was who had built this cavern? He honestly had no clear answers to any of the questions. It was his first day in the cavern, and already there were questions he could not answer. When he got back to the ATV, he pulled out the solar stove and got it ready to boil water for dinner. While he was waiting for the water to boil, he decided to fly the drone three hundred feet in the air to film the lake below. Once the drone was high enough, he set it on hover, and made sure it was not over the lake, just in case. He kept his smart glasses on, so he could keep an eye on the lake while the drone was hovering. It took thirty minutes for his water to boil, and during that time he saw nothing move in the water. He let the drone hover while eating dinner. After dinner was over, he still had not seen anything move. By this point he was doubting that he had seen anything move. There were still a couple more hours before heading to bed so decided to keep the drone hovering. Part of him wanted the camera to see something, and another part of him was afraid it would see something.

Once Raymond had eaten, he walked back up to the top terrace to inspect the cavern wall closer. After reaching the top he walked along the wall in the opposite direction he had earlier to see if he could find anything different. An hour later, every garden he walked by had the same doorway shape in the wall. He counted twenty-six gardens as he walked along the wall, and they all looked the same. Occasionally, he touched the wall where the dark line was, but never felt a crack, or a line in the crystal. The only possible explanation was the lines were decorations. He headed downhill towards the lakeshore, and back to the ATV. While he was walking, he watched the feed from the drone on the smart glasses. The drone had been hovering for hours and had not seen anything move in the lake. No doubt, thought Raymond, there was nothing in the water. Being alone in this large cavern must be playing tricks on my mind. It was past 8 PM as he walked back to camp, and it would be time for bed soon.

By the time he reached the ATV, it was almost 8:00 PM, and Raymond started getting ready for bed. The temperature had been holding a constant 76 degrees all day, which meant he did not need to dress warmly to sleep. Because of the earlier scare from the water, he decided to wear his pants while in the sleeping bag. He wanted to be prepared in the event of a fast escape. He knew it was silly, and a bit of an overreaction, but it was always better to be safe than sorry. While stowing the solar stove, and the few things that were out, it became obvious darkness was setting in. It was now a little after 8:00 PM, which showed Raymond the cavern appeared to be on a twelve-hour cycle. Twelve hours of dark and twelve hours of light. Raymond knew plants did best in a twelve-hour cycle, especially during their flowering season. Before it got too dark, it was wise to pull out the solar lights and finish getting ready for the night. At least it was going to be comfortably dark to sleep, he thought.

By 8:30 it was as though a full moon was shining inside the cavern. It was light enough to walk around and not run into things. Before climbing into bed Raymond grabbed his headlamp and phone. Stella made him promise to call her every night before going to sleep. She said, it was not as good as a goodnight kiss, but at least she would know he was safe. Even though they had talked earlier she was happy to hear his voice. He told her about walking further down the wall looking at the lines. She said the cavern was amazing and agreed the lines must be for decoration. Is it possible for you to transmit the pictures from the drone while it was flying, so she could watch while he was exploring, she asked? Not a problem, he answered. The plan is to have it fly above me tomorrow while I am driving. The flight today was so fast that it might have missed key details. He left out that he was using the drone to look for the shadow he had seen in the water earlier. She was nervous enough he was exploring the cavern alone, without having to worry about shadows. After talking for a while, they said goodnight, and he settled back and thought about the day.

After talking to Stella, it was only 9:30 PM which meant he still had 11 hours before it was daylight in the cavern. Raymond grabbed his smart glasses, connected to the Internet and started doing research on the plants that he had seen today. Four or five of the berry plants he saw on the internet were like the ones growing in the cavern. His guess was whoever had built the cavern had hybrid the berry plants to grow here. He was certain if they had not been hybrid, they would have overgrown the cavern. Most berry plants growing wild, or in a garden environment, spread like a weed. The berry plants in the cavern, as well as every other plant he had seen, seem to have a controlled growth rate. How could every garden he came across in the cavern, not spread like in nature unless they were hybrids? Raymond was a man who liked answers, and answers were hard to come by in this cavern. He was not happy, Stella wanted to watch the feed from the drone. His plan was to fly the drone overhead while he was driving the ATV to keep an eye on the lake. If by chance, there really was something in the water, and the drone photographed it, he really did not want Stella to see it. He knew if she saw something moving quickly in the water, she would be worried and want him to leave the cavern. Sometime, just before midnight, Raymond fell asleep.

When he slept Raymond did not usually remember his dreams. Tonight was different. Raymond woke up at 7:30 in the morning and lay there thinking about the dreams he had that night. He had dreams of things flying in the water, weird plants, strange doors that opened in the side of the cavern, and large birds chasing his drone. If he did remember dreams, it was only one or two of them, they were simple, and not weird like last night's. In hindsight he should have brought someone with him, but he did not know who he could trust. When Mike finds out he came down here alone, he will yell at him for hours. He knew he could trust Mike, but he was also afraid that something might happen to him just like it happened to Papa and Kirk. Mike was his best friend and the thought that something had happened to Mike was not acceptable. Raymond could see it was starting to get light in the cavern. It was just after eight in the morning, and in thirty minutes, it would be full daylight, so he got up, and started preparing to cook breakfast. By the time he got everything ready for breakfast it was fully light, and he set up his solar stove to boil his water. The freeze-dried meals he brought were great tasting, especially the scrambled eggs with sausage. Today was going to be another long day so along with the scrambled eggs, and sausage he decided to cook up oatmeal as well. While he was waiting for the water to boil, he walked up to the terrace and picked a handful of berries. After trying the berries yesterday with no ill effects, he decided to try more this morning, but only a small handful. The berries tasted wonderful and having them on his oatmeal would make the morning start off better.

While he was walking up to the terrace, he called Stella to say good morning. She said she was still in bed and apologized for being lazy that morning. Raymond told her he could not get up much earlier because it was not full light in the cavern until 8:30. She said, some people would like that. "Twelve hours of dark every night would be an easy way to become lazy," she said. He agreed and told her he was up picking two or three berries to try on his breakfast that morning. "Be careful of those berries," she said. Do not worry honey, he said I am only going to have one or two every day just to be cautious. "Please be careful Raymond, I would hate to have to come down there myself and find you," she said. Honestly, honey, if you had tasted these berries, you would understand why I like them so much. "Just remember you promised to bring me berries when you come back so I can try them," she said. "As much as I like these berries myself, you can bet I am bringing a bunch back," said Raymond. He let her know what his plans were for the day and that he would be streaming the video from the drone while it was flying. After their conversation he picked the berries for his morning breakfast and headed back down to the ATV.

The water was boiling when he got back, and Raymond began making breakfast. He really liked the scrambled eggs and sausage, but the oatmeal made breakfast a winner. While he was eating the oatmeal he wondered if it would be possible to bring the berry plants home to plant in his garden. As wonderful as they tasted he bet he could make a fortune growing these berries and selling them in stores. He even thought about asking the guys at the Boeing lab if they wanted to go in with him to start a berry farm. They could even call it the Cavern Berry Farm, he mused. After eating breakfast, he cleaned everything up, packed it away, and got ready for a long day's drive. After five hours straight driving yesterday Raymond was tired, and decided today, he would break it up into at least two separate rides. His plan was to ride until lunchtime, take a couple of hours break, then head out again until dinnertime. He had twelve full hours of light, so he was not in a hurry.

Once he had everything stowed in the trailer and made sure it was secure, he prepared the drone for the day's first flight. While he was getting the drone ready for the morning flight, he decided to call Tony Baker, the man he got the drone from, to ask if it was possible to have one of the cameras only send the data to his smart glasses. Raymond did not want Stella to worry, so he needed to find a way to film the lake to see if there was anything in it but not let Stella see it so she would not worry.

Tony picked it up right away, and Raymond explained he would like to have the data from one of the cameras sent only to his glasses and stored in the drone's memory. Tony said it really was not a problem and explained how to do it. He really did feel guilty about hiding this from Stella, but knew it was better, so she would not be worried about him. Tony explained all he had to do was set one of the cameras to stream to wherever it was he wanted it streamed. Once he had the computer set to stream only the information he wanted to send to Stella's computer, he finished preparing the drone for flight. He programmed the drone to fly in automatic mode, at an altitude of five-hundred feet in front of him and five-hundred feet above him. That height would allow the drone to film things before he got there. That altitude was high enough it had an unobstructed view in the event there was anything moving in the lake. Once the drone started, he watched it fly up. Once the drone reached its altitude and distance in front of him it stopped and hovered. Satisfied that the drone was working perfectly Raymond got on the ATV and started driving down the cavern.

With the drone leading the way, Raymond drove the ATV 20 miles an hour down the cavern. He had all day and there was no reason to hurry, and at that speed it was easier to observe things along the way. After an hour Raymond shut down the ATV and walked up onto the terrace. The gardens here looked identical to the gardens where he had stopped for the night. He walked up all the way to the top terrace and over to the cavern wall. He wanted to see that the cavern wall here had those same door shapes. He was not surprised that the gardens here had identical door shaped decoration in them. Once his curiosity was satisfied, he headed back down to the ATV and continued driving down the cavern. The drone had been perfectly leading the way and sending the camera feed from the lake camera to his glasses. He was happy that he had not seen anything moving in the lake, but it still made him wonder. Was there something there or was his mind playing tricks on him the other day. He had not heard from Stella yet that morning while he was driving and assumed she was busy doing something else. When she started watching he was sure she would say something to him. She was just as amazed with the cavern as he was and was sure she wanted to be there with him. When another hour of riding had passed, Raymond took a break again. There was still nothing unusual in the gardens above, or the water, but he knew he should take a rest.

Raymond had stopped by the lakeshore this time so he could rest near the water. He needed a little different scenery and was not as fearful of the water anymore. He grabbed a snack out of the trailer and took his shoes and socks off and dangled his feet in the water. The water felt good, and he even thought about taking a sponge bath. He now had been in the cavern for over 24 hours and was sure he needed a bath due to the stress he had been under. He was eating his snack daydreaming, looking into the water when suddenly something huge went by in the water below him. Raymond jumped up so fast he almost fell back into the lake. Whatever was in there, it was big, and it was moving fast. It looked to be the size of a large commercial jet, and he could swear it was going just as fast underwater. Now he was sure he had seen something yesterday. Whatever this thing was, he knew it was not alive because nothing living could travel that fast. He backed quickly away from the lake and stood behind the ATV honestly shaking. He could not figure out what could move that fast underwater. It did not appear to be far underwater, but it was not making any sort of wake, or even a ripple on top of the water. Whatever it was it paid no attention to him. Knowing that made him feel better, but he still could not figure out what it was. Suddenly, it dawned on him he had not seen a thing in the heads-up display in his smart glasses.

He looked up and saw the drone was still hovering where it should be, and he was getting the feed from it in his heads-up display, but he had not seen anything. Raymond took the remote control off the ATV and backed up the camera feed that was filming the lake. He replayed the camera feed half a dozen times, but he could not see a thing in the water. The water was clear, and whatever it was, was close enough to the surface Raymond could see it, so he was certain that the high-tech camera on the drone should have been able to see it. His mind was now racing hundreds of miles an hour trying to figure out what was going on. He had no other choice but to call Tony again and see if he had any idea what was happening. He could not tell him where he was, or what he was filming, so he had to think of a way to explain the problem. When Tony answered, Raymond explained that he had seen something move under the water in a lake, but the camera on the drone did not pick it up. Raymond then asked him if there was any reason the camera would not film something underwater that he could see with his own eyes. After Raymond's question, Tony was silent for a couple of minutes. Then, Raymond heard Tony ask somebody if they had any idea why.

Tony came back on the line and asked Raymond to hold on while they had a meeting to see if they could produce a reason for the the camera's failure. Raymond sat listening for the next 10 minutes as Tony and his lab personnel talked and argued. When Tony came back on the phone, he apologized for taking so long and said that honestly, they had no idea why the camera could not pick something up that Raymond could see with his own eyes. He added that the cameras on the drone were so high tech, even if a bright light had been shining directly into the camera, the software would have been able to see through it. He also said water was no problem because the software would enable the camera, even in cloudy water, to see almost one thousand feet deep. He went on to say the drone was for the military and could see a submarine in salt water at least one thousand feet deep. The only reason they could think of why the camera failed to pick up the object was an incredibly sophisticated blocking system. Tony went on to say that as far as he and his lab personnel knew, no one in the world had anything that sophisticated enough to block the camera, and software built into the drone. I know you are secretive about what you are exploring Raymond but is there any chance you can tell me where you are, and what you think you saw?

"I am sorry Tony, I really cannot," said Raymond.

"I didn't think so," said Tony. "I promise you the guys in the lab, and I will keep working on the problem. If we produce something I will get back to you," Tony added.

"Thanks," said Raymond, and if I have any more questions, I will call you.

Raymond stood behind the ATV for another half hour trying to decide what to do. It seemed obvious whatever was in the water either had not seen him or was not interested. With that in mind he decided to continue exploring the cavern, and from now on he was going to ride close to the lake to see if he could see whatever it was again. Before he started driving, he decided to eat something and call Stella. He wanted to make sure everything was all right at home and let her know he was doing fine. When she answered, she explained she had been outside with Grandma. Grandma did not usually go outside, but today she was feeling energetic, and wanted to go sit in the sun. She knew Raymond was gone, and assumed he was trying to figure out what had happened to Papa. Somehow that knowledge made her feel better. When Stella asked how things were going Raymond said fine and that nothing was different or unusual today.

He told her he felt fine after eating the berries in his oatmeal, and he was considering taking a sponge bath in the lake. She said after all the work he had been doing, it was wise nobody else was with him, and taking a bath would be nice. Raymond called her a stinker. They talked for a while longer, then said goodbye. Raymond had stopped for more than two hours and thought it best to get going again. He still had over eight hours of daylight left, really had no schedule, but after seeing that thing underwater again, decided it was best to move on.

Raymond got back on the ATV, double checked that the drone was still flying above and started driving down the cavern again. He kept the ATV about ten feet from the water's edge, and this time kept the speed down to ten miles an hour. Being that close to the edge of the water he did not want to take any chance of falling in. He knew if the ATV and the trailer went in the water, he would have a heck of a time making it the sixty miles back to the shaft. While he was driving next to the shoreline, Raymond thought to himself, ten miles an hour on an ATV seems fast, when you were surprised as he was. Also, having no other way out of the cavern, keeping the ATV on dry land was a great idea. Before he came down next time he was going to see if Mike could outfit the ATV, and its trailer with pontoons. After driving for another hour, he stopped the ATV to take another break. He knew he should take a break every hour even though he was only driving ten miles an hour. He grabbed a thermos of water, an energy bar, then stood looking into the lake. He was not afraid of what was in the water, but he was going to be cautious until he could figure out what it was. He had not seen anything moving in the lake by the time he finished his snack, then got back under way.

He had been driving for about forty minutes, when something went by him in the water again. He almost drove the ATV into the lake as it passed. If he had not been going so slow, he was sure he would have ended up in the water. It is odd, he thought, whatever was in the water went in the opposite direction this time. Why was it going in the same direction he was? For a moment, he considered heading back home. If it were not for the fact that he did not feel threatened, he would have. It would be nice to have somebody along to help dissipate the nervousness right now. He stopped and shut off the ATV. He had not seen anything in his heads-up display but wanted to play back the film to see if he had somehow missed it. Just like last time, nothing showed up on the camera. Since whatever it was, went in the same direction he had been going, he had more time to see it with his own eyes. Now, there was no doubt something was in the water, which was big and fast. Tony's assumption had to be right. Somehow, whatever it was, could block their high-tech equipment. There is no point in contacting Tony's lab again because there was nothing they could do to help. Also, no sense getting him curious, and having to fend off more questions until he was ready. Raymond watched the replay a couple more times, then decided to keep going. Experience has now shown him, the camera equipment was not going to pick up whatever is in the water, so no sense wasting anymore time. Time to get back on the ATV and continue.

Raymond knew he had not driven far that day, but with all the excitement he didn't care. This was only his second day, and he still had almost two weeks before he planned to leave. No sense worrying about speed, or distance at this time, he decided. He started the ATV, and made sure the drone was hovering properly above, and took off again down the cavern. Driving at 10 miles an hour meant he was not going to do one hundred miles a day but felt safer. The plan was to drive for two more hours, then stop for the night. After an hour he stopped the ATV, this time over by the hill, and away from the lake. He had enough excitement for the day, and really did not want to take another chance of seeing whatever was in the water. Raymond wanted to stretch his legs a little bit, so he walked up the terraces to look at the plants and check out the cavern wall. The plants looked slightly different but not too noticeable. He tried a couple of the berries, and they tasted just as good as the ones before. After trying the berries, he walked over to the cavern wall to see if the doorway design was there as well. He was not surprised the cavern wall was identical to what it had been before. The doorway design appeared to look the same, and when he touched the lines, they were smooth with no indication of any sort of crack or indent. He thought to himself the plants, and the cavern wall might seem boring being so consistent. The consistency was better than the thing moving in the water, he thought. He walked back down to the ATV and prepared to leave for his last hour drive.

He decided to drive next to the lake again, but this time mentally prepared himself for his underwater surprise visitor. After making sure the drone was hovering properly and the radio signal to the controller was good, he got on the ATV and started going. He kept an eye on the water, but for the whole hour drive, he kept going over, and over in his mind what had transpired that day. Raymond was certain without photographic proof no one would believe what he had been seeing in the water. If he had not seen it so many times, he would not believe it himself. He knew unless one stopped and let him take a picture of it even, he would have a tough time believing it. He did not know how to make somebody believe him without proof. For now, he knew it was best to not say a thing to anyone. He had to keep exploring the cavern in the hopes he would find proof. He was relieved when he reached the end of his last hour drive that nothing else had happened. It was just after 6:00 PM when he stopped the ATV. He picked up the remote for the drone and landed it next to the ATV for the night. Once the ATV shut down and secured for the night, he pulled out his solar stove to boil water for his dinner. With the water boiling he got the trailer ready for his night's sleep. While he was waiting for the water to boil Raymond went over to the lake to fill up his water jug. He knew the water had been assessed pure enough to drink, but always ran it through the filter just to be doubly sure. While filling his water jug Raymond made the decision that after dinner he was going to come back to the lake and take a sponge bath.

After dinner and cleanup, it was a little past 7:00 PM and he was running out of time before it got dark. He grabbed clean clothes, a washrag, and headed over to the lake. Raymond enjoyed camping, and he and Stella went as often as they could. While they were camping, they refrained from using any sort of soap to preserve nature.

Tonight, was no different than any other night camping. He was going to take a sponge bath with no soap. Honestly, the last thing he wanted was to have soap in his hands and see that massive thing move underwater in front of him. If that happened, he knew he would have dropped the soap anyway. He was grateful that this water was much warmer than a mountain stream. Taking a bath in a cold mountain stream is almost painful. Freezing water is fine in the morning when washing your face, but taking a bath is never fun. Raymond stood at the water's edge looking down praying he did not see anything. He stripped off his clothes, dipped his rag in the water, and started washing. Unlike most places he goes camping, taking a sponge bath here meant he did not need to worry about somebody watching, or accidentally seeing him naked. That thought made him smile and wonder what would happen if the thing in the water saw him naked. Would they be so surprised they crashed, or would they just laugh at the site? His luck held out. He was able to take a bath without anything or anyone going by. All clean and fresh Raymond headed back to the trailer to get ready for sleep. After he called Stella of course.

It was past 8:00 PM, and just starting to get dark, when Raymond climbed into the trailer for the night. He had a busy day today filled with excitement. He could not talk to Stella about the thing in the water. If she had been with him when he saw the thing in the water, she would understand there was not much to worry about. If he tried to talk to her about it, she would insist he came back home, and he could not do that. She picked it up immediately when he called and was in a great mood. Spending time with Grandma outside made her happy. She told him she was amazed at how well Grandma was doing, and how healthy she looked. Honestly, she said she has not seemed this happy, or healthy in the last 20 years we have been here. Stella had told her Raymond was out looking for signs of Papa. Now, she said Grandma was not sad, she seemed incredibly happy instead. Raymond told her he thought she felt happy because finally she would be able to get closure on what happened to Papa if he was successful. Stella agreed and said she was just grateful to see

Grandma so happy. He told her about his day minus the thing in the water. She reminded him again not to eat too many of the berries, regardless of how wonderful they tasted. Also told him to remember to bring berries back for her. By the time he got off the phone it was dark in the cavern. He looked up at the bar of light in the ceiling of the cavern and wondered who could have built this marvelous place. He knew when he finished exploring, he was going to have to find experts to come in and help explore this cavern. He was sure it would take years, and every scientific discipline to explore it. Who had the technology to build something so fantastic? There were hundreds of wondrous things, he thought. The cavern walls, the hybrid plants, and the light at the top of the cavern were just three. With those thoughts in his mind, Raymond fell into a deep sleep for the night.

When he finally woke up in the morning it was light out in the cavern. He could not believe that he had slept for over ten hours that night. It was unusual for him to sleep even eight hours in a night let alone ten. Obviously, the stress from the two days before had finally caught up with him. While lying in bed, he marveled at how wonderful he felt. After yesterday's events he thought he would feel tired or stressed but instead this morning he felt energized. He had not put in more than one-hundred miles on the ATV, but it discovered amazing things. He still did not know what was in the water, and could not tell anyone about it, but at least he knew he was not in danger from it. Raymond climbed out of bed, looked around the cavern with wonder and began getting ready for the day. The first order of business was going to be a big breakfast. Usually in the morning he is not that hungry and eats because he knows he should. He pulled out the box with all the food in it, picked a scrambled egg with sausage pack, and an oatmeal one as well. Since it was already full light, and he was hungry, Raymond set up the solar stove to boil his water for the morning breakfast. While waiting for the water to boil he walked up onto the terrace with the intent of picking a small handful of berries for his oatmeal. After picking the berries he walked around and looked at the gardens and marveled at how beautiful they were. While walking around he absentmindedly ate all the berries that he had picked. By the time he realized he had eaten the berries it was too late. He had filled his coffee cup with berries and eaten the whole cup full.

He stood there amazed at what he had done. He knew better than to eat a handful of berries at one time, not knowing for sure if they were safe. Although he had eaten berries the previous two days with no adverse effects, he was a little worried. The more he thought about it the less worried he was. If he were going to have any sort of reaction from the berries it would have already happened. The lab checked the samples of plants he had brought including the berries and found them to be perfect for human consumption. Because nothing that he came up against in this cavern was harmful to humans he decided not to worry and filled his cup up again. He felt certain that if the berries were going to make him sick, he would already be sick. And to be honest the berries tasted better than the freeze-dried food he brought along. With another full cup of berries in hand Raymond walked back to the ATV to fix this morning's breakfast. Even though he had already eaten a cup full of berries he added the new cup to his oatmeal and ate it like a man starving. After eating his oatmeal, he dared not tell his wife of berries he devoured. When everything was clean and put away Raymond called Stella for their morning talk.

Stella sounded just as happy this morning as she was last night. She told Raymond she missed him but was grateful he was trying to find out answers for Grandma. He let her know his plans for the day, and how amazing it was to have the opportunity to explore this cavern. She told him, next time he went down, she was going also. She was not going to let him leave her home alone when he went on such an incredible adventure anymore. It was nice to be able to look at the videos, she said, but being there with him would be more fun. She also told him when he got back, he better have Mike build her an ATV just like his. He promised her he would have Mike build her one, or one they can sit side-by-side on. Stella said she liked that idea especially since he had been gone too long already. After a while she said she had to get off the phone, she heard Grandma calling and said goodbye. After the call ended, he packed everything into the trailer and prepared for the morning ride. After yesterday's excitement along the waterfront, the decision to stay right at the base of the hill was a smart one. No sense taking a chance of driving into the lake, he thought. When the trailer and the ATV were ready Raymond started up the drone and set it to hover above like it was yesterday.

He thought about driving up to the top terrace following the cavern wall today but decided against it. Even though the ATV had big soft tires he was afraid it would damage the plants. The gardens look so beautiful and perfect the thought of damaging them was unthinkable. Even though ten miles an hour was not going to get him extremely far fast, he decided to stay with that speed. He was not in a hurry and was able to examine things in greater detail at that slower speed. With the drone hovering above, Raymond climbed onboard the ATV and started down the cavern. After an hour riding, he pulled over to rest. Plants by the cavern looked identical to the ones he had seen the last few stops, so he did not go up to check on them. After a short stop and a cup of coffee he was on his way again. The next hour's ride was also uneventful and being away from the water's edge kept him from seeing anything that might be in the water. While he was sitting there resting Raymond switched cameras in his heads-up display. When he got to the camera that was focused on the plants alongside the cavern wall something caught his eye. It was not something obvious like something that looked a little different. He decided to walk up and see for himself.

Once he got to the top terrace he began looking around. At first, he did not notice anything that was different. Then, it dawned on him two of the plants were an assorted color and looked a little taller. Three of the berries had different shapes than other berries he had seen before. A couple of the berries looked yellow instead of red and blue like the ones he had seen before. On closer examination one of the berries had a yellow tint. He picked one and looked at it closely. The lab had not assessed any yellow berries, so he decided to be cautious and try a nibble. To his surprise it tasted a little bit like a banana. He was not sure if it was just his mind tricking him, so he ate the rest of the berry. It tasted like the other berries but had a slight banana taste to it. He was positive the berries would be fine to eat, but for now decided to be safe, and not eat anymore. He was sure whoever built this cavern would not have included anything harmful to humans because they had not so far. While looking at the berries something else was nagging at him. He was not sure what it was but something else seemed different. Raymond stood and slowly looked around the terrace to try to figure out what it was. Then it dawned on him, the door shaped decorative lines on the cavern wall were darker. They were darker enough he could tell once he looked at them closely. He walked over and ran his fingers over the line. He could not feel the line or a depression, but they were darker. Not too different, but it was the first change in these lines he had seen throughout the cavern exploration. From now on he would remember to keep a closer eye on these lines to look for any more changes. With that he headed back down to the ATV to start riding again.

Raymond decided to ride along the waterfront again. He was curious if whatever was under the water was on a schedule or was it random and wanted to try to time its appearances. Even though the drone could not film the mystery watercraft he decided to keep the camera on it regardless. Though he might have missed the craft already because half the morning he had ridden below the terrace, he decided to start timing anyway. It was more enjoyable to ride next to the water. After an hour's ride he had not seen a thing in the water, pulled over to take a rest, and eat lunch. He felt especially hungry today, which he thought was odd considering all he had been doing was riding an ATV. He pulled the solar stove out, filled it with water and placed it in the sun to heat it up. Next, he rifled through his box of food and pulled out a lasagna dinner. This lasagna dinner was a meal for three, which made him smile, because it made him feel like a teenager again with the kind of hunger he felt. He knew Stella would comment and warn him he would get fat eating like that. While waiting for the stove to boil his water Raymond walked up the hill to the top terrace to look around. He grabbed the remote for the drone because he wanted to have the drone take close-up pictures of the cavern wall, and plants.

While walking up the terraces he noticed the plants along the way were in fact different than the ones earlier in the cavern. He flew the drone down closer to the ground to get close-up pictures of the plants. Even though he had his smart glasses on pictures and movies he knew the cameras on the drone were much better. He was sure the lab would be delighted at seeing the change in these plants as he progressed down the cavern. When he finished taking pictures of the plants, he continued to the cavern wall. After noticing that the lines in the doorway design had been getting darker, he knew he had to take pictures of those as well. Once he reached the cavern wall, he was glad he brought the drone because the lines were darker than they were earlier this morning. When the drone had finished taking pictures of the lines in the cavern wall, he flew it back up to its hovering position. With the drone at a higher altitude, it was able to get a better view of the cavern for future reference. Raymond walked over to the plants that looked different to take a closer look. The plants were obviously larger than the ones earlier in the cavern. The color of the berries in this area were also different. There were more yellow berries than he had seen earlier that morning. While he was looking closely at the berries, Stella, who had obviously been watching quietly suddenly said, oh those are pretty.

Raymond had been concentrating deeply and jumped when she spoke. He must have also uttered something improper, because she started laughing immediately. I am so sorry Raymond, she said still laughing. Stella, you almost made me pee my pants, he said. Raymond sat down and started laughing at himself. Oh my God Stella, I was concentrating so hard and did not realize you were watching. Next time would you please be a little louder, he asked. Stella was still laughing, and said she had tears in her eyes. "I must admit being down here alone does make me a little jumpy," said Raymond. It took a couple minutes before both could settle down and stop laughing. I know it was at your expense, but that was the best laugh I have had in a long time, said Stella. "Glad I could help," he said. "Those plants really are pretty," she said. "I was looking at them closer because I noticed the berries were an unusual color," said

Raymond. "Can you have the camera get a closer look, so I can have a better look," she asked. Not a problem, give me a second to get the drone down here. He flew the drone down to within twenty feet of the ground and had the camera on the yellow plants. He did not dare get any closer, or the air coming off the propellers would blow the plants around too much.

"You are right," she said, these berries do look a bit more yellow than any of the berries I had seen before." "I thought so too," said Raymond. They taste different also. I tried one this morning and it had a slight banana taste. "Did you say banana," she asked? Yes, they still taste like sweet berries, but with a slight taste of banana in the background. Raymond, you better promise to bring me yellow berries when you come back home. "Will do" he replied. "Please do me one more favor Raymond," she asked. Anything dear, what would you like? "Would you give me a close-up of that dark door shaped line in the cavern wall please," she asked?

Raymond focused one of the drone's cameras onto the wall, and zoomed in. Is it me Raymond, or does it look like the line is a crack? He was wearing his smart-glasses and used them to zoom in closer to the dark line. You know Stella, it really does look like it is a crack. He walked over to the wall and ran his fingers along the line. "Well, I'll be," he said, "it feels like this line is a crack." Stella watched as Raymond walked along the cavern wall feeling the dark lines. "Good eyes Stella. You were right about it being a crack now," he said. "What do you think that means," she asked? "I don't have a clue, he said." Up until now they were dark lines we thought were for decoration, and now these appear to be cracks. "I truly do not have an idea what is going on," he said. "Earlier today I noticed they were darker but did not appear to have any sort of crack," said Raymond. There are more questions than answers in this strange cavern. "Looks like I am going to need to pay a little closer attention as I proceed further down," said Raymond. "Just be careful," she added. "Grandma already lost Papa, and I would hate to have something happen to you, honey," she said. "You do not have to worry about me being careful, especially after my little scare minutes ago," he said. Stella made a little chuckle and promised to inform Raymond next time she was watching. "As humorous as it was, she did not want to scare him again," she said. "I really appreciate that," he answered. Now it's time for me to get back on my way. I have more exploring to do here.

Stella said goodbye, told him she had to see how Grandma was, and she would look in on him a little later. Raymond flew the drone back up to its hovering point and walked down to the ATV. On the way down he kept thinking about the dark lines, and why they now had a crack. There really were more questions than answers down here. This was one of those times he wished somebody were down here with him, so he could ask questions, and feel less nervous. He grabbed his water, an energy bar, and ate a snack before getting on the ATV. He decided to ride for an hour and then stop for lunch. Checking out the cavern wall and talking to Stella had taken a while but wanted to get in more riding before he stopped to eat. Even with the little scare from Stella, he chose to continue riding next to the lake. It was important to keep looking for whatever was in the water and try to get a time schedule, if it was on one. Just hope if I see it again, I do not drive into the lake, thought Raymond. After about twenty minutes riding, something flashed by in the water. To his credit, this time when it went by, he did not jump. Was he getting calloused, he wondered? He made note of the time and kept driving for another forty minutes, then stopped for lunch.

After setting up the solar stove, he went to sit by the lake shore to think. Why were the plants on the cavern wall changing, and what did it really mean? There really were so many questions that needed to be answered. He was going to be grateful for the time he could ask experts his questions. He had seen incredible things inside the cavern, but he still had not seen any sign of Papa and Kirk. All the things he had seen in almost three days of riding, added questions but no answers. If it were not for all the excitement, he was sure he would be frustrated. The plan was to ride for another five days then turn around if he had not found any sign of Papa and Kirk. If he did not find any signs of what happened to Papa, Grandma was going to be devastated. To be honest, he was amazed he had not seen any sign that either one of them had been in the cavern. His hope was that they had survived the trip down the shaft and somehow, were able to survive. The cavern was warm, and had food, water, and light. There was everything a human needed to survive, so he still had hopes of finding signs they had been there. When he first got in the cavern, he had to decide which way to go. If at the end of his two weeks he still had not found any sign of the two men, he was going to have to come back down and go the other way. If he had to come back and go the other direction, he was certain Stella was going to demand she come along. The more he thought about it, the more he liked the idea of Stella being along. The cavern was beautiful, so far it was safe, and it would be nice to have someone else with him. After eating lunch, cleaning up, and putting everything away, Raymond got back on the ATV to head down to the cavern again.

He had been riding for an hour, and was preparing to stop for a rest, when again, something huge flew by him under the water. This time it was heading the same direction he was, which gave him a little more time to see it. Whatever it was traveled so fast it was impossible to determine what it was. All he could tell was it was large and amazingly fast. His best guess was it was the size of a large jet airplane. He was still amazed that something that large could go that fast underwater, and not leave any sort of wake or ripple. He had now seen it enough times to know for sure if it was real, even though the cameras on the drone could not pick it up. This underwater anomaly was one of the reasons Raymond would like someone along. He stopped the ATV and sat for five minutes to think. He was wondering if he should not turn the ATV around and head the other direction, since he had not seen any sign of the two men yet. He got off the ATV and walked down the shoreline trying to decide what to do. He chose to keep going in the same direction for the rest of the week if he had not found anything before then. He knew the cavern held everything the two men would need to survive and was certain they would have continued walking until they found something, if they had been alive. They must be alive he thought, otherwise he would have seen signs that they had died. Since he had not seen any bones or bodies it seemed obvious to him that they had survived the accident at the bottom of the shaft. He also had not seen any signs of wildlife that would have eaten their remains, which gave him hope they had survived. There was no sense thinking the worst about the men, so he turned around, and went back to the ATV. It was 3:00 PM which gave him another three hours riding time before stopping for the night.

The next hour of riding was uneventful. Nothing went by in the water, the plants, and the cavern walls looked the same as they did a couple of hours ago. He stopped the ATV, pulled out his water, a protein bar and sat by the lake. After a short rest Raymond got back on the ATV and continued driving. He was surprised over the next hour riding, nothing unusual happened. Over the last three days he had been surprised so many times it would not be a surprise if something happened again, he thought. When he stopped for his rest break, he decided to head back up to the cavern wall and inspect it. The plants along the way looked identical to what he had seen when he was talking to Stella earlier. The dark door shaped lines were just as dark, and when he felt them, they felt the same. The cracks in the cavern wall were a big mystery. His imagination was running wild thinking what the cracks were for. While inspecting the cracks closely something caught his attention out of the corner of his eye further down the cavern. The sight down the cavern shocked him. For the first time in three days there was something different in the cavern. The minor changes in the plants and the cavern wall were nothing compared to what he was seeing. Something quite different was down the cavern, but too far away to tell exactly what it was. From where he stood it almost looked like the end of the cavern. The zoom on his smart glasses was not strong enough to be able to discern what it was. Raymond almost ran down to the ATV to get the remote control for the drone.

He picked up the remote control after getting to the ATV and turned the cameras straight down the cavern. Even with full zoom he could not get a clear picture of what it was. He remembered Tony had told him the zoom was only good for ten miles, which meant whatever he was seeing was much farther away. He was frustrated that the camera was only good for ten miles even at full zoom and decided he was going to invest in Tony's company so they could get a better zoom. He was excited and decided to call Stella. He wanted to let her know that he had found the end of the cavern. After three rings she picked up, asked how he was doing, and what he called for. Raymond was so excited he had trouble talking. Because he was having such a tough time talking Stella was worried that something was wrong. She kept asking if he was OK while he was stammering trying to get his words out. Finally, he said no, everything is fine, everything is fine. Are you sure, she asked? Absolutely Stella, it could not be better. "Raymond, what are you trying to tell me," she asked? "I think I found the end of the cavern," he said. "That is great," she said. Well, honestly Stella, it is the end. The camera on the drone can only zoom ten miles, and this is much further so it cannot get a clear enough picture to know for sure. This is the first time that the inside of the cavern has looked different in the last three days, he said. Well, what are you going to do, she asked? My only option is to drive further down the cavern until I can get close enough to fly the drone to get close-up pictures, he said.

Raymond explained the drone's remote only had a range of fifty miles. Best he could tell, whatever he was seeing down the cavern had to be twice that far. He explained distances inside the cavern were difficult to determine, because it was so straight and flat. The plan was to keep driving down the cavern tomorrow, to see how close he could get. He told her he was still going to keep the speed down in the ATV, so he would not miss anything along the way. There had been no sign of Papa or Kirk yet, but he was not going to hurry and take a chance on missing anything. Stella agreed that was a promising idea, since he still had four days before he needed to turn back. She thanked him for calling and said to make sure he called at bedtime. Raymond was extremely excited, and although he did not expect to find Papa or Kirk alive, he was hoping to find signs that they had made it to the end of the cavern. He had talked to Stella for over an hour, and it was now well past six o'clock, which meant it was time to stop for the night. After landing the drone and securing it for the night, he set up the solar oven to start his water heating. Once he had the solar oven set up, he got the trailer ready for bed. He was so excited he really was not sure if he was going to be able to sleep that night. He knew it would be a long day tomorrow, and he had to try his best to calm down, so he could sleep. It looked like he was going to need all the rest he could get.

He was too excited and decided to walk up to the cavern wall to drain his excess energy. It would not have mattered if the plants were different, or if one of the door-shaped decorations opened. He was so excited he would not have noticed it anyway. After walking around absentmindedly Raymond headed back down to the ATV to have dinner. He grabbed a package of freeze-dried macaroni and cheese, then poured hot water into the pouch. Ten minutes after eating, he would not have been able to tell anyone what he had had for dinner since his mind was elsewhere. After dinner he grabbed a rag, clean clothes, and went over to the lake. He had time before he needed to climb into his sleeping bag and decided on taking a sponge bath. A bath was the best way to spend the extra time. With all the excitement he was quite sure he needed one.

Until Raymond took his shirt off, he had not realized how dirty he was. At that moment he was grateful Stella was not there. She was always teasing him about taking more showers or wearing more deodorant. Sometimes he worked too hard and did not have a chance to take a shower. At least that was one good thing about being down in the cavern alone, nobody complained if he was stinky. After a shower he made sure the drone was secure for the night and stowed all the extra gear. With an hour to go before it was dark, he decided to take a walk up to the cavern wall. He did not have a desire to look at plants or inspect the wall, he just wanted to walk. Tomorrow is going to be a big day. He could not be sure what he saw down the cavern was the end, but it was something different than he had seen over the last three days. Three days, he thought. He had been down there for three days in a cavern no one else knew about, except Stella that is. He had seen things no one else had ever seen, at least in modern times. He still had no idea what was going back and forth in the lake.

He wondered who, or what was inside that, large, dark, fast-moving shape. While standing on the top terrace, Raymond stared at the anomaly far down the cavern. He could not be certain how far away it was, but he was guessing it was going to take him at least two days on the ATV to get there.

As much as he wanted to get there as fast as he could, it was wiser to be cautious, and not miss a thing. Once he was under way in the morning, he would send the drone out until it reached its limit, then turn back around, and fly back autonomously. The hope was the drone could get close enough to take pictures that were good enough, he could identify what was down there. If it could not reach the anomaly tomorrow, he was certain it could be the next day. After looking further down the cavern for a while, Raymond walked down to the trailer to get ready for bed. While walking, he thought how enjoyable this cavern would be with Stella by his side. He even imagined what it would be like to build a house down here. There was food, water, light, and the temperatures were comfortable. The worst part about this place he imagined the weather could get boring. Boring that is if you did not like 76 degrees every day. It was still light in the cavern when Raymond changed clothes and got ready to climb into bed. He still needed to speak to Stella, so after he climbed into his sleeping bag, he gave her a call. They talked about tomorrow's plans, and she told him how excited she was, that they would find out what happened to Papa and Kirk. After a short talk they said goodnight and Raymond settled in. He still was not tired and ready for sleep, so he lay there with his eyes closed, and relaxed.

He did not remember falling asleep, so when he awoke in the morning, he was surprised how quickly he had fallen asleep the night before. It was 7 AM when he woke up which meant he had an hour before it started to get light. While he was lying there, he called Stella to see if she was awake. She answered right away and told him that she had been awake for over an hour. "I just could not sleep well last night," she said. I kept imagining that somehow when you get to the end of the cavern, you would find out what happened to Papa and Kirk. "I keep hoping the same thing," he said. "I promise if I can't find out what happened to him at the end of the cavern, I will head back the other way to find the opposite end of the cavern," he said. They had only been talking for five minutes when Stella said she had to get off because she heard Grandma calling. "She would talk to him later," she said. She also made him promise that as soon as he learned something he would call her right away. "I promise honey," he said, "I will call you as soon as I know. something." Even though it was dark out Raymond got up to stretch his legs. He was going to grab his headlamp and make coffee when something caught his attention down cavern. He realized far down the cavern, possibly, where the anomaly was, it was light. Because it was still dark in the cavern where he was, he was able to see how much brighter it was further down. He stared down there looking at the light wondering what it was. The light intrigued him, and he looked at it as the cavern began to become light again. Afterwards, he was sure there was something down there, it was not his imagination. With a new sense of hope he pulled out the solar stove to prepare breakfast.

After breakfast he stowed all his gear and secured the trailer for travel. Once the trailer and the ATV were ready to travel, he prepared the drone for its first flight of the morning. He decided to drive along the base of the hill, instead of next to the water, because he knew he was going to be spending lots of time looking further down the cavern and did'nt want to take a chance on driving into the lake. Once he had the drone in the air he got on the ATV and started driving. This morning, he planned to drive two hours before his first stop. He knew he could drive even more, but decided caution was the best course of action. If he were not alone, he would be taking more chances. At the end of the two hours, he stopped the ATV and got off for a rest. After stopping the ATV, he sent the drone ahead at full speed.

The drone could fly at two hundred miles an hour, but only had a range of fifty miles before the transmitter lost contact, and the drone would return. At top speed it would only take the drone 15 minutes before it reached its maximum range and returned to Raymond. While the drone was flying ahead Raymond grabbed an energy bar, and water, then went to sit by the lake. He was wearing his smart glasses and watched the drone speed ahead. By the time the drone reached its maximum range and turned around, Raymond couldn't tell what the anomaly was even at full zoom. He was a little disappointed, but decided not to waste any more time, and got on the ATV to meet the drone on its way back.

Fifteen minutes later the drone was hovering above. There is no sense sending the drone out again until further down the cavern, he thought. It was best to ride another two hours before trying the drone again. By that time, he would be hungry, and he could eat lunch while sending the drone out once again. He grabbed his water, and an energy bar, then got back on the ATV. After another two hours Raymond had now traveled approximately forty miles since starting off that morning. He stopped the ATV and sent the drone out at full speed one more time. Once the drone was flying, he took out the solar oven to boil water and waited. Fifteen minutes later the drone again reached its maximum distance and was beginning to return. The drone was now ninety miles further than where he started in the morning but was still unable to tell what that thing was further down the cavern. While the drone was flying back, he replayed the film and realized the reason he could not tell what the anomaly was. It was like the anomaly was not there. Not so much blacked out, but he couldn't see it in the pictures at all. It was like the problem the cameras had with what was in the water. It could not photograph what was at the end of the cavern. It was like the area was invisible. Now, he was really confused. What is causing the cameras to malfunction or block their ability to take pictures? Tony had to be right. Somehow, something was able to block the camera's electronics, but by who or what?

It was obvious he had no other choice but to drive to the anomaly and see what it was with his own eyes. When he finished lunch and had everything stowed away, he called Stella. Raymond told her about the light further down the cavern that morning when it was still dark. She couldn't understand why the camera was not able to photograph the anomaly and he told her he didn't understand either.

He told her that he talked to Tony, the man he got the drone from, and that Tony suggested there was something blocking the cameras electronics. Stella suggested that whoever built the caverns was obviously technologically highly advanced. "There must be a reason for secrecy," she said. Raymond said he agreed, although he couldn't understand for what reason. Before she said goodbye, she made him again promise to be careful. He said he would, and explained he was going to drive for the next two hours at 20 miles per hour, to see how close he could get. Since he still hadn't seen any sign of Papa or Kirk, he was not concerned about driving fast today, he told her. He didn't believe there would be any signs, and felt it was better to get to the anomaly. If they had lived, he told her, he was sure they would try to make it to the anomaly, and that is where he would find any sign they had been there. They said goodbye and he left immediately. After two hours of driving, Raymond could tell the anomaly was closer. The cameras on the drone still couldn't photograph the anomaly, but he could see it better with his eyes. He was not close enough to tell what it was and decided to drive for another two hours. It was 4:30 in the afternoon, so if he drove for another two hours he would still have two hours of light to fix dinner before it got dark.

For the last two hours while he was driving, he could see the anomaly getting bigger as time went by. It was now 6:30 in the evening, and he had driven one hundred miles that day. He could not tell for sure exactly what was there, but it looked like the end of the cavern. Because of the size of the cavern, distances were hard to judge. From where he was standing, he was certain he would be able to make it to the end within two or three hours the next morning. He parked the ATV and landed the drone for the night. For the first time since he set foot in the cavern, he was tired and ready to stop. He set up the solar stove and got the trailer ready for the night's sleep. While the water was heating, he grabbed a washrag and clean clothes, then went over to the lake to clean up. Eight hours of riding the ATV with almost no rest left him tired and feeling dirty. If it were not for the strange thing in the lake, he would have jumped in this time. Until he knew what was in the water there was no way he was jumping. When he got back to the ATV, he fixed his dinner and sat down and relaxed. It was almost 8:00 o'clock and in 30 minutes, it would be dark. He was tired but wanted to stay up until it was fully dark, so he could get a good look at the anomaly. While driving today he didn't talk to Stella because he wanted to make suitable time. Once it got dark, he was going to call her and tell her what he saw at the end of the cavern.

At 8:30 Raymond put his smart glasses on and called Stella. He was hoping the glasses would be able to photograph the anomaly, but to his dismay they couldn't take a picture. He told her what he could see and how close he was. "I really wish I could see what you see," she said. So do I, said Raymond. It is quite beautiful. I am now close enough to see it tapers down into a smaller opening than the two-mile-wide cavern. There seems to be quite a bit of light coming out of a room, or a smaller opening. "Sounds fantastic," she said. I wish I could be there with you Raymond. "I do too, to be honest I am a little nervous," he said. Not scared, just slightly nervous. I would be scared if there had been anything threatening in the cavern during my time here, he said. It almost feels like I am nervous seeing something beautiful, like the Grand Canyon. It is magnificent, majestic, and slightly intimidating because of its potential. "What do you mean," she asked? It's like that feeling you get when you are standing against the railing of a tall bridge. You feel safe, you know you are not going to fall, but the height and the view makes you a little uneasy. "I understand what you mean," she said. "Like feeling overwhelmed," she added. "Exactly," said Raymond. "Honey, I am tired, and need to get up early tomorrow, so I am going to say goodbye for the night," he said. "Not a problem my dear husband," she said. Sleep well and I will talk with you in the morning. After they hung up Raymond sat for a while looking at the light further down the cavern. He knew tomorrow was going to bring the answers they had been looking for. He just didn't know what they were going to be.

After looking at the lights the night before, he had gone to bed about 9:30. When he woke up it was 6:30 in the morning and he still had two hours before full light. He peeked outside the trailer and saw light coming from the end of the cavern. He lay back down and thought about what the day was going to bring.

Part of him didn't want to go down to the end in case he did find signs of Papa and Kirk. He was also so curious about what was down there he could hardly wait to get going. Even though the drone might not be useful for taking pictures, he decided to keep it flying as it had been before. The drone had been capturing pictures of the plants and especially the cavern wall for later inspection. He hoped once he got close to that area at the end of the cavern the cameras would work. He would not bet money the cameras would work, but he had to keep them rolling just in case. Looking at the lights this morning he was hopeful it would not take long to get there. The plan was to continue going at twenty miles an hour so he could get there quicker. At first light Raymond got up and prepared breakfast. While breakfast was cooking, he called Stella to fill her in on the plans for the day. After talking to Stella, eating breakfast, and stowing all the gear, he was ready to travel.

As he was driving towards the end of the cavern, he could see more detail with every mile. By the time he reached his two-hour mark he could tell that it was the end of the cavern. Even from this distance, he could see the ceiling and walls slowly curved inward and down towards a small opening. Although small, in reference to the size of the cavern, it might be big. He was unsure how far away it was and wished he brought binoculars. The best guess Raymond could come up with was the end of the cavern is close enough to make it within the next hour. After a short break Raymond got back on the ATV to continue down the cavern. After forty minutes he slowed the ATV back to ten miles an hour. It now looked like he was less than a mile away from the opening. He was not sure whether he was feeling scared or excited about what he was seeing, and what he might find. He stopped completely when he was one hundred feet from the opening. He sat and studied the opening for five minutes. From this distance the opening overall was one hundred feet tall and one hundred feet wide. There appeared to be openings on both sides of the lake. From here he could not tell whether the lake ended or went under the wall. Either way the wall stretched completely across the one-mile-wide lake. Raymond sat and marveled at the engineering needed to create such an incredible thing. He could not be sure because of the distance, but there appeared to be something inside the opening.

After sitting for what seemed like hours staring, he started forward again. He slowed down to just barely a walking pace marveling at the site. He realized the drone was still flying at five hundred feet and flew it down to twenty feet off the cavern floor. No sense taking a chance on running into the cavern wall, thought Raymond. He had his smart glasses on but still could not get any pictures of the end of the cavern wall. When he was about one-fourth mile from the wall the drone slowly sank to the cavern floor and stopped. When the drone landed, the camera feed to the smart glasses stopped also. He stopped the ATV, picked up the remote for the drone, and tried getting it started again. No matter what he did the drone would not turn on. He had been flying it five hundred feet in front of the ATV when it sank to the floor. Raymond was slightly concerned that the drone had stopped, but slowly drove the ATV forward to get a closer look. While driving forward he kept an eye on the opening at the end of the cavern. He told himself if he saw something he was going to turn around and drive at full speed in the other direction. The moment he pulled alongside the drone the ATV shut off completely. There was no way this was a coincidence, thought Raymond. He tried turning the ATV on and off two times with no success. The ATV was dead. At that moment he realized his smart glasses had also stopped working. Now he was starting to get nervous. He pulled his phone out of his pocket to call Stella. His phone was also dead. No, he was not just nervous, he was scared. He sat on the ATV for two minutes trying to decide what to do. He thought about getting off the ATV and running back the way he came but realized that it was almost two hundred miles. He only had one option, he had to walk in the opening and see what was there.

9

THE CENTER HUB

Finally, Raymond got off the ATV, and slowly walked forward. He was not sure what to expect, and as he walked, every one of his senses was in overdrive. He could see that the area beyond the opening was not empty. There were shapes and lights he could see throughout the area inside. He paused just outside the opening and looked around. He looked behind him and all around making sure there was not anything, or anybody close. Inside the opening was a huge room. All throughout the room were large walls that had writing and glowing screens like computers. Once he was sure no one was inside he stepped in. He was half expecting the opening to close behind him, thankfully it did not. Slowly he stepped forward looking at the different patterns on the walls. They looked like pictures on a normal computer screen, but they were like lights on the wall, and he could not see a normal computer screen. The shapes, colors and symbols just seemed to appear on the wall. Raymond had never seen anything like it. Even in science fiction movies they had computer screens. Who created technology like this? The shapes on the wall look familiar, he thought. There were plants, birds, and bugs. The shapes he could not identify at all might have been letters. His guess was those shapes are a language. If the camera and phone were still working, he could take pictures. He didn't even have a pencil or paper to make copies of them. Every day there were more questions and no answers, thought Raymond.

No one, or no thing, had jumped out, so he continued to search the room. The room was the size of a large store. The ceiling must have been over fifty feet tall. With all the walls, he couldn't see how big the room was. His only option was to keep walking to see what he could find out. Everywhere he walked, the walls had light patterns or pictures. None of it makes sense, he thought. For all he knew this could be a library, a museum, or even a control room. When Raymond walked in, he was careful to keep track of where he had come from, which was a clever idea as he was starting to get hungry. It looks like investigating this room will take hours if not days, so he walked back to the ATV to eat lunch and plan. He was relieved when he turned the corner and saw the ATV down the cavern. He knew no one was there, but his biggest fear was the ATV would be missing. He walked to the ATV and pulled out his solar stove to prepare lunch. While the water was heating, he walked over to the lakeshore and sat down. He had things to think about. Being lonely made it worse for him. The drone was not working. The ATV was not working, and his phone was not working. It would be difficult to be in a worse situation than he was currently in. There did not appear to be any other option than continuing to search the room. Being unsure how big the room was, he needed to make sure to stay alert. He had to find a way to always find his way back. Although there was food and water in the cavern, it was wise to carry a backpack with supplies.

He went back to the now, dead ATV, to fix lunch. After he finished lunch Raymond started going through the trailer looking for anything that would help him. It was too bad the trailer didn't have four wheels so he could have easily pulled it like a wagon. If there is a chance of getting out of here, and coming back, it would be with a trailer with four wheels he could pull. He did not like the idea of not having a running vehicle and traveling with so few supplies. Raymond pulled everything out of the trailer and laid it on the ground. It was the best way to itemize what he had and make the best decisions. While unloading the trailer he wondered what kind of technology could knock out every piece of electronic equipment. He could not even call Tony to ask if he had any ideas. He was not up a creek without a paddle, he was at the top of a waterfall. For the first time he was having doubts about making it out of this cavern. That thought made him wonder if Papa and Kirk had also felt the same way, if they survived the fall. He told himself they must have survived the fall, or there would have been signs in the debris pile. The idea they may have made it this far made him feel better. With everything laid out on the ground, Raymond started looking at his supplies and devising a plan.

The first thing he did was separate out all the food. If he was going to have to walk, food was going to be the most important thing, next to water. With the food separated, he pulled out everything that could hold water. He had enough food to last at least three weeks, if rationed. The lake disappeared beneath the wall under the room. Since he had not seen any sign of water in the large room, he needed a supply for exploring further. He would need to carry enough for drinking and cooking. He had four closeable containers that could hold water. He decided to empty the food bin and use it to carry water. He estimated that the bin could hold ten gallons of water, which would be too heavy to carry. He needed to find a way to pull the water behind him. It was warm enough inside, so he did not have to worry about bringing all his clothes. He picked five pairs of socks, two changes of underwear, and a coat. He knew he could go weeks without changing underwear, if he was all alone, but clean socks were vital to protecting his feet in the event he had to walk for days. He had food, water, and clothes, now he needed to figure out a way to carry it. The floor of the cavern is smooth, so he could easily slide, or pull things across it, Raymond thought. The sleeping bag had a tear resistant nylon backing, and although he did not need it to sleep in, it would be perfect for pulling things across the floor. Next, he had to figure out a way to pull the sleeping bag across the floor loaded with his gear.

He decided to use the nylon strapping from a tiedown to make a tow rope, which he would attach to the backpack. The backpack has padded shoulder straps, and waistbelt, which would act like a harness, so he could pull the sleeping bag behind him. When he saw the roll of tape, and a small spool of green twine, he got an idea. He would use them to mark his way through the room to avoid getting lost. Until he explored, there was no idea the size of the room. By cutting small pieces of the green twine, and taping it either to the floor, or a wall at intersections, he could find his way back to the ATV. The size of the large room was unknown, but he could not take the chance of getting lost. Now that he had his food, water, and a way to avoid getting lost, Raymond was feeling confident. He took the food bin and water containers to the lake and filled them. He was paranoid, he thought, but better to be safe, he reminded himself. With the supplies loaded onto the sleeping bag, and the harness attached to the backpack, he walked back towards the large room.

The first thing he did was tape a short piece of green twine to the wall at the entry. His idea was to tape a piece of twine at every corner he turned. From his first visit he knew the large room was a maze of walls and corners. He wanted the ability to turn around and see where he had come from. He had no idea how big this room was and wanted to avoid getting lost. Raymond was intrigued by the glowing writing on the walls and decided to investigate towards the center of the room first. There were too many walls coming out of the sides that prevented him from walking the perimeter first. He was also curious about what was in the center of the room. He expected the perimeter to be laid out like a normal room in an office or computer center. Offices, and computer centers have infrastructure on the outside, and the important items in the center. If this room was a museum, or computer center, he expected to find the most interesting aspects in the center of the room. Raymond knew it could take multiple tries to find the center of the room and came up with a plan. For his first attempt he would walk in on the left-hand side, then turn right. He knew if every time he came to a wall and turned right, eventually he should come back to the point where he came in. If not, he could turn around going back to the left, and he would end up where he started.

After taping the twine to the wall Raymond headed to the right and followed the wall, always keeping to the right side. With all the left and right turns, it was impossible to know how far he walked before reaching the same entrance where he came in. He was grateful for the green twine, because it was visible as he rounded the corner at the other end of the room. Now he had a good idea of the size of the room, and how to proceed. On the next attempt, he would begin on this right end, walk in one aisle further and keep to the left. After taping twine to the wall, Raymond walked down the next aisle always keeping left. It worked again. He had come out against the far wall, looked to his left and saw his green twine taped to the wall. Now he knew his plan would work and it would be near impossible to get lost. With that knowledge, Raymond walked back to the cavern, took off his backpack, and left his supplies outside. Without hauling all the gear, it was going to be much easier to explore the room. With only his tape, and twine, he walked back in to continue his exploration. Without the anxiety of getting lost he was able to concentrate more on the glowing figures on the walls. After 20 trips to the right, and twenty trips to the left Raymond was becoming tired, and hungry. He followed the twine back to the entrance for lunch, and a much-needed rest.

Since now he knew he would not get lost Raymond hauled every-thing back to the ATV to load up the trailer once again. He was unsure how long the exploration of the room would take but decided to sleep every night in the trailer. He set up the solar stove to boil water for lunch and loaded everything back into the trailer. When finished with loading the trailer, he grabbed clean clothes, a washrag, and walked to the lake for a bath. He was thinking about what he had seen in the room while bathing when the huge underwater anomaly sped by. He was so startled; he fell into the lake. If anybody had been there and seen what had happened, they would have fallen to the ground laughing in hysterics. He must have looked like a cat that fell into a bathtub frantically trying to claw his way out. He can laugh about it now, but at the time he was sure he would get eaten by whatever it was in the water. It was the first time he had gone into the water rather than taking a sponge bath. It took over an hour before he calmed down enough to remember he had his solar stove boiling water for lunch. If the ATV could run, he would have left immediately. Raymond had never been so scared in his life. Being alone in this cavern was stressful enough without falling into a lake with something unknown and huge in it. When he calmed down enough, he fixed lunch and ate it. He was too tired and too shaken up after falling into the lake to continue exploring the room. Instead of exploring he walked back down the cavern to relax and try to get his head straight again.

He had been walking about fifteen minutes, when a voice suddenly came out of nowhere asking if he was OK. He was still on edge after the incident in the lake, and jumped ten feet, yelling loudly. The voice came from the phone in his pocket. While preparing for his trip into the room, he had forgotten to take the phone out. He was grateful the phone had been left in his pocket, because for an unknown reason it was now working. It was Stella's voice that scared him. Raymond pulled out the phone and stared at it. The phone was always on intercom, so they could always hear each other. They kept it that way as a safety feature in the event of an emergency in the cavern. When he could finally concentrate, he realized Stella was asking if he was OK. When he assured her that he was, she kept asking why he didn't answer her earlier. Raymond explained, as he approached the large room at the end of the cavern that the drone, the ATV, and his phone had all died. "If I had not had the phone in my pocket while taking this walk, I would not have known the phone was working," he said.

'Do you think if you push the ATV away from the room it might work also," she asked? "You know Stella, that is a great idea," said Raymond. "I will try it when I get back." he added

Raymond told her about exploring the big room using tape and green twine. "Smart idea," she said, "I don't want you getting lost down there, and not coming back to me. He then told her after exploring for a while, he went back out to the ATV for lunch. Without thinking he told her about getting scared and falling in the lake. Stella's reaction to him being scared by something in the lake reminded him he was not supposed to tell her about the lake anomaly. To say she was upset would be the understatement of the year. She went on for at least five minutes berating him, and reminding him, how she would kill him, if something happened to him down there. Raymond apologized and told her he did not want her to worry unnecessarily. After seeing the thing in the water enough times, he had realized it was not a danger. She reminded him, if it was not really a danger, he should have told her. He gave his word to never hold another thing back while down in the cavern. "What do you mean, down in the cavern," she asked? "You better mean, every time, from now on my dear man." With that comment they were both finally able to laugh.

Raymond started walking back to the ATV, while he was talking to Stella, and suggested they keep talking until the phone went out. Once it stopped working, he would back up until the phone started working again. "Great idea," she said. He was about twenty feet from the ATV, when the phone died. He turned around and walked back another ten feet and heard her talking again. Raymond suggested he push the ATV back to where the phone started working, to see if it would start working also. "Sounds like a good plan," she said. He said the phone was going off again, but suggested she keep talking, so he would know when to try the ATV. He was barely able to push the ATV with the trailer. The hard work reminded him to have Mike make a trailer with four wheels, so it could be pulled like a wagon in an emergency. Luckily, he only needed to push the ATV about thirty feet before he heard Stella's voice again. Just to be sure, he pushed yet another fifty feet to make sure there would not be a problem. He told Stella what he was doing while pushing because she heard grunting, groaning, and asked what was going on. Once he stopped, he climbed onto the ATV, and sure enough everything was working again. Raymond was relieved and knew he would be able to get out of the cavern again without having to walk. He told Stella she was a genius, and if they were not already married, he would marry her. He said he was going to camp there, and not head back into the room until morning. When they finished talking, he got the trailer prepared for the night, and relaxed.

After the tiring morning, and moving equipment, it was three in the afternoon. With five hours of light left, Raymond decided to walk up to the cavern wall, and relax. The view this close to the end of the cavern was incredible. Whoever built this cavern had fantastic technology. The curve from the top, and sides of the cavern to the room was a mile, yet somehow the curves were perfect. Raymond had been staring at the end of the cavern for almost 20 minutes when he realized something was different. He stood up and looked around and then he saw it. The plants were different. There were more red berries at this end of the cavern but that isn't what stood out the most. The door shaped design in the cavern wall now looked more like a door than a design. Earlier in the cavern the dark line felt like a crack. Now without even touching the line he could tell it was a deep crack. Now more than ever the door design looked like an actual door. After everything they had gone through that day, he felt afraid to walk over to the door for fear that it would open. After five minutes of debating what to do, Raymond stepped up to the wall and looked closely. From two feet away it was obvious the crack went deep. He broke a stem off one of the plants at his feet and inserted it into the crack. It went in about four inches before it stopped. He slid the stem all the way to the ground in the crack and then as far up as he could reach. He walked over to the other side of the crack and did the same thing. There was no doubt this design had become some sort of door. He looked all around the walls but could not see any method to open the door. He tried pushing on it to no avail, it would not move. He wanted to show Stella, but he didn't have his smart glasses with him. He decided that before he called Stella he would go down and get his glasses, so she could see for herself.

On the way back from picking up the glasses he called Stella. She answered before he reached the top terrace. The first thing she asked was "are you OK honey?"

"I am fine dear," he said, "but there is something here I think you really would be interested in seeing. His smart glasses were transmitting as he was walking up the hill and she saw the plants as he was walking by.

"Raymond, I know you think the plants are interesting, but I am too busy right now to look at them," she said. "Hold your horses little one," he said, "I am there." He stepped up to the wall and turned to look at the deep crack in the wall. "Oh my," she said, "is that what I think it is?" "Is that a deep crack now," she added? "It sure is Stella. Since you noticed the crack first, I thought you would enjoy seeing what it looked like now," he said. "Oh my, it looks like a door now," said Stella. I checked the crack out closely, and it goes about four inches deep, on both sides as far as I can reach. "Do you think it's a door," she asked? "Not sure what it is," said Raymond. "I looked everywhere for a way to open it and even pushed on it," he said. "There does not appear to be any handle or button to push or pull to open it," he said. "If not a door, what do you think it is," she asked? "Honestly, I'm not sure; an unfinished door, or a change in the design," he added. As you always say Raymond, questions, and no answers. "Well, whatever it is, it is another mystery in the cavern for later discovery," he said. Thank you for sharing, now I need to get Grandma back in the house. "She has been outside for two hours, and goes out every day, since you went down into the cavern," said Stella. "Call you later," said Raymond.

After the call, he sat on the top terrace thinking about the unanswered questions that have been piling up. While deep in thought, he didn't notice immediately he was getting rained on. He was concentrating on how the lake disappeared under the room. He had not looked completely throughout the room, but there was no sign of water inside. When a large drop of water landed on his nose, then another hit his glasses, and went into his eye, he came back to reality. "Oh my god," he said aloud, "rain! I can't believe there is rain falling." He stood and looked up to the cavern ceiling. His face received a cascade of warm drops as he stared upwards. The phone in his pocket let out a loud, "what," from Stella. "Looks like you are correct again my dear," he said, "the rain is falling." "That is incredible," she said. "Raymond, hold on while I go into the computer room to watch," she said. "I am not holding on," he said, "I need to get out of this rain." The rain was beginning to fall harder, and he started walking back to the ATV for shelter. By the time he was halfway down the terraces the rain was coming down heavy. He was almost running now and could hear Stella laughing. "Good thing I have a covered trailer," said Raymond. He was laughing along with Stella as he reached the ATV and jumped into the trailer.

The trailer is meant for hauling gear and sleeping in. There was barely enough room for Raymond to sleep, and changing out of wet clothes was an impossibility. While he was changing, Stella kept calling him a chicken, and told him to go back out, so she could enjoy the rain. "Not on your life," he said, "the rain is warm, but it is coming down hard." "Oh, come on Raymond, you know you need to shower," she said laughing. "If you were here misses," he said, "I would make sure you were outside to enjoy it yourself." With a bit of effort, and amidst Stella's laughing, he was able to change into dry clothes. He had not brought any rain gear, so he grabbed a large garbage bag, and made a poncho. With the impromptu raincoat and hat, Raymond stepped back outside into the warm rain. They both watched the rain falling inside the cavern with wonder. As suddenly as it started, the rain stopped. Raymond guessed it rained for fifteen minutes. Fifteen minutes of hard rain. He used his smart glasses to zoom in on the terraces. "You are right again Stella," he said. The depressions around the gardens were filled with water running slowly downhill towards the lake. "Well, that is one mystery solved," she said. Now we know how the plants get watered. "It's a good thing the rain stopped," said Raymond, "otherwise I would be eating a cold dinner tonight." "At least you finally had a shower," said Stella. "All right funny girl, time for me to start making dinner, now that the rain has stopped," he said. "Talk to you later, Rain Man," Stella said with a giggle.

While Raymond was pulling out his solar stove, he was grateful he repacked the trailer, otherwise everything would have been soaked. Once the stove was set up Raymond took off his garbage bag poncho and stowed it within easy reach in the event it started to rain again. With the water heating, Raymond walked to the base of the hills to check the water runoff. *Whoever built this place really knew what they were doing*, he thought. The small depressions around the gardens were the perfect size to hold the rainwater runoff, without overflowing. Raymond looked up toward the top of the cavern and zoomed in with the smart glasses. He couldn't see where the rain came from. Well, the mystery of how the plants get watered is solved, but where the water comes from is a new mystery. So many questions and so few answers, thought Raymond. He walked back to the ATV to eat dinner and reflect on the day. After dinner he headed over to the lake shore to relax. It was 6:00 PM and he had two more hours before it would begin to get dark. He was sitting for twenty minutes when the lake anomaly flashed by him going toward the room he had been exploring earlier. To his surprise he did not even jump when it cruised. Considering how he had fallen in the lake earlier; he was amazed how calm he felt. So today he thought, I had a bath, and a shower inside a huge cavern two miles underground. After sitting a while longer Raymond got up and walked over toward the large room. Tomorrow is giving me a long day, and decided to bring lunch in the backpack, so he could explore longer. He was looking at the lake under the wall of the large room, imagining how far it went, and what was underneath, when he realized it was beginning to get dark. He headed back to the trailer to get ready for bed and talk to Stella one more time.

Being so exhausted from the grueling day, he immediately fell asleep. When he woke in the morning, he couldn't remember any dreams, and he had only just laid down. It was still dark when he woke up. His watch said it was seven o'clock. He slept for over ten hours. Being so early in the morning, he was worried about waking Stella, so lay in the dark thinking about the day ahead. With no idea how big the room was, but knowing he needed to explore faster, it was time to change plans. Today he would walk in on the left wall and turn left every time he came to a wall. Walking this way, he would be sure to stay along the outside wall of the room. Using this method, following the outside wall, he should come out of the opening he went in. At least if it were a single room, he thought. It was starting to get light and was after 8:00 o'clock. He climbed out of the trailer to get things ready to make breakfast, once it was fully light. While he was pulling things out for breakfast and exploring the room later that day, Raymond called Stella. She answered right away and asked how he was doing that morning. He told her he slept dreamless straight through the night, and now felt fully rested. After explaining what the exploration plans were for the day, they said their goodbyes, and he set about making breakfast. While the water was heating, he gathered the gear needed for the day including a large lunch. The ceiling in the room was one hundred feet high but was not lit by the same light as the cavern ceiling. The whole ceiling seemed to glow but did not have a center light. He is unsure whether it will be able to heat his water, so packed energy bars and dried fruit.

While eating breakfast he decided his lunch was going to be boring, so when he finished, he grabbed one of his sealable containers and went up to the terraces. The berries would be delicious, and so far, he had felt no ill effects from eating them. While he was filling his container, Raymond ate a couple of handfuls. With a container full of delicious berries, he headed back to the ATV to put on his gear for his exploration. Before leaving, he called Stella once more, to tell her he would be out of communication for half the day. She made him promise to be careful and said she would be waiting for his call. When the call was over, he put on his backpack and walked back toward the expansive room. Even though the plan is to follow the wall always keeping to the left, he decided to bring his tape and twine, so that he could mark his path occasionally. The plan was simple, and it should have been impossible to get lost, but being alone in the cavern he needed to be sure. He stood outside the entrance of the room staring inside for a minute, took a deep breath, and headed in. He followed the plan by keeping to the left wall and following it at each turn. Every ten minutes he taped a piece of that twine to the wall. He knew the twine was overkill, but it made him feel more secure. Ever since he was a kid, he loved hiking in the woods alone. Except for an occasional scare from a bear, he never felt uncomfortable alone, even in the deepest woods. With so many unusual things in the cavern, he can honestly say, this was the first time he felt uncomfortable alone. Not being able to talk to Stella or anyone else makes it tougher, he thought. Raymond had snacked a bit as he was walking, and by noon he was feeling a bit tired, and hungry, so decided to stop for lunch.

After a thirty-minute lunch, and rest break, he started walking again. He knew he could walk two more hours, turn around, and still get back while it was light. The lights never went off in this room, so he was not worried, even if it meant he had to stay after dark. His concern was getting overly tired and having to sleep uncomfortably in the room for the night. Next time he came in, he decided he was going to carry his sleeping bag, and pad, with extra supplies in case he needed to stay the night. After walking twenty minutes, Raymond had just finished taping pieces of twine to the wall, walked around a corner, and stepped out into an incredibly large domed ceiling room. To say he was surprised would be the understatement of the week. The room was unbelievably huge. It was then he noticed he had gone through an opening that was at least one hundred feet wide. The ceiling inside the domed room was at least a mile high and appeared to be two miles wide in either direction. He stood at the entrance studying it. It was just as wide and tall as the cavern he had been down in for days. Glancing around he could see tall walls with glowing pictures like the room he had just been in. In this room the walls were shorter, only twenty feet tall. The walls were only in the center of the large room. From where he was, he could not see any walls near the outside of the dome. He couldn't tell for sure, but it appeared there were openings on either side of the room identical to the one he was standing in. In the very center of the domed room, between the walls, was a huge glowing ball. He was too far away to make out what the ball was, but from this distance, he could tell it was rotating. The walls in the center looked like they were a half mile wide, and it was a mile to the walls with the rotating ball in the center. He could not tell for sure, but the rotating ball looked like it was as big as the walls below. That meant the ball must be one-half mile across.

Raymond did not feel comfortable walking out into the middle of the domed room. Something about that huge glowing ball rotating in midair scared him. Instead of walking out to the center of the room, he walked to his left to investigate the opening on that side. When he walked out into the room towards the opening, he could see the opening he had come out of was in the center of the wall. The wall was two miles wide, which was just as wide as the cavern he had been in for days. He angled sharply to the wall on his left, staying as far away from the center of the room as possible. After fifteen minutes walking, he reached the opening on the left wall. As he got closer, He could see through the opening, and saw it was identical to the room he came out of. He did not go in, instead he stood looking around then glanced across the large dome room. As he expected, the side opposite the one he came out of also had a large opening. Raymond was unsure what to do. He was nervous, and tired. He decided the best course of action was to head back the way he had come and talk to Stella. He wanted her input, but also needed to talk to her to calm down a bit. If his phone and cameras were working, he would feel less nervous. He turned around and quickly walked back to the opening he had come out of. He was walking fast, and tried to slow his pace a bit, but his nerves would not let him. He had spent almost two hours out in a large room, and it was a little after three o'clock by the time he got back to the room. When he was safely inside, he followed the wall back the way he had come. He ate berries, and a couple of energy bars on the way back but did not stop until reaching the cavern.

Raymond was overwhelmed with a sense of relief as he walked back into the cavern. Over the last five days he had seen incredible things, but the domed room today beat them all. Once he reached the ATV, he needed to call Stella and let her know he was OK. What he had seen today was so incredible he was not sure if he could describe it to her. The closer he got to the ATV, the more he relaxed. The feelings of fear, and doom, were gone, replaced by a sense of wonder. By the time he reached the ATV he was exhausted and sat down. He needed awhile to gather his thoughts. After ten minutes sitting quietly, Raymond put his smart glasses on to call Stella. It is after six and she answered immediately. As expected, her first question was are you OK Raymond? "Yes, I am fine," he said. His silence after that comment made her nervous, and she asked again, "are you sure you are OK?" Truly Stella, everything is OK. I have things to tell you, I am just not sure where to start, or how to describe what I saw today. "Oh god, did you find Papa and Kirk" she asked? No, I promise it was not anything bad, it was incredible. I followed the walls like I told you I would and finally found the end of the room. "That's great Raymond," she said. "Don't hold back honey, tell me what you saw," she added. When I reached the end of the room, it led to another room that was bigger. It was bigger than anything I could have ever imagined.

Raymond spent the next hour trying to describe what he had seen to Stella. During the whole time Stella only said a couple of words, and never once asked a question. After we finished talking, we were both silent for what seemed like an eternity. I wish you had been with me Stella; it was so beautiful it is impossible to describe. I wish you could have seen it. "Promise me you will take me down next time Raymond, please," she asked. I promise you Stella, I do not ever want to come down here alone again, and you deserve to see the cavern, and all the wonders inside. "Thank you, Raymond," she said. He finally told her he was exhausted, needed to cook dinner, and promised he would call at bedtime. After saying goodbye, he set up the solar stove and started preparing dinner. While preparing dinner, he played what he had seen over in his mind. When he finished dinner, he went over and sat on the first terrace to relax. After the day he had, the last thing he needed to do was sit down by the lake and be startled by the underwater anomaly. He knew that tomorrow he had to check out the giant rotating ball in the center of the domed room. He did not know why, but of all the things that he had been through in the cavern, this made him the most nervous. He was not sure if he were afraid that he would find the remains of Papa and Kirk, or if it was something else. He knew in his heart Papa and Kirk were gone, and he was prepared to find their remains. What he was not prepared for was the technology he might find in the center of the room. From a distance, seeing that gigantic ball floating in midair, and rotating was not so much scary, but intimidating. He realized it made him feel small, and insignificant. Whoever had built the cavern was so far beyond human technology it was impossible to comprehend. When he finally went to bed his dreams were filled with images he had seen that day before.

Raymond woke up the next morning, and automatically went through his morning routine, and prepared to leave for the dome. After talking to Stella and assuring her that he would be careful he headed out. This time he walked straight through the room and in just over 2 hours reached the domed room. He stood at the entrance staring across to the large rotating ball, while he pulled out his tape and twine. He hung pieces of tape and twine around the entrance of the room, then walked towards the center of the Dome. With the room entrance marked, he only needed a couple of arrows near the center of the dome pointing back to his room. If he got turned around while he was out in the center, all he needed to do was walk around until he found his arrows pointing back to the room. Two hundred feet from the first wall in the center Raymond taped two arrows on the ground pointing back towards his room. He walked forward one hundred feet and put down two more arrows. With the arrows down on the ground he walked up to the wall. To his right he could see a door about four hundred feet away and walked toward it. When he reached the doorway, he stood outside and looked in. This room was very different from the room he had walked through. Instead of a maze of walls with glowing symbols, it was simply four long walls with doors every so often that made the square, with a floating ball above. Raymond laid a couple of long strips of tape along the floor, then taped twine on the edge of the doorway. He realized there was not much chance of getting turned around but did not want to take that chance.

The four long walls that outlined this large room were covered in the same indecipherable glowing symbols, and pictures as the other rooms. Now that he was standing underneath the rotating ball, he was able to make out details. At first all Raymond could see were glowing lines and darker shapes. The more he watched, the more he realized he was recognizing some of the shapes. He realized he was feeling too tired and hungry to think and decided to rest and eat before trying to concentrate further on the ball. He took off his pack, sat on the floor, pulled out his water, and food, and started eating. While eating, he lay down on his back and looked up at the rotating ball. The ball was huge and was not rotating fast, which took a while before he saw even a fraction of it. The longer he lay there the more he realized it looked familiar. There was something about the dark lines that were familiar. He was certain the ball was at least half mile across, and at the speed it was rotating, could take a couple of hours for one full rotation. He was unsure how long he had been watching the ball rotate, when it dawned on him, he knew what it was. It was a huge model of the earth. Once he realized what he was looking at he was able to identify the first continent, then the second. Now he really wished Stella were with him. She would be ecstatic at the discovery. Raymond lay back for another hour watching the giant earth rotate above him.

He now knew that the dark lines represented the continents on earth. What he could not figure out was what all the glowing lines crisscrossing across the globe were. It was not until it rotated to the North American continent, and the United States, that he had an idea. When it rotated so Washington State was directly above, he knew exactly what the lines were. He got up, started jumping and yelling, "I have it, I have it." He was grateful no one was around, because he was sure he looked like a crazy person. He did not care anymore, because now he knew exactly what those lines were. When the globe rotated around to Washington State, he recognized that one of those glowing lines went right under Tenino Washington. The glowing lines were caverns. He looked back at the earth and studied the drawing lines closer. What he realized was the glowing lines intersected each other. At every intersection there was a dot. At every intersection there were four glowing lines and one dot. He realized at that moment he was inside one of the dots. He had come in one line into the dot, and there were three lines leaving the dot. That meant there were three other caverns leaving this dot. There were thousands of lines all over the earth. There were lines under the continents, and under the oceans. He could not believe what he was seeing. The earth was covered with these caverns. He laid back down on the floor staring up at the globe. As he was looking, he realized the rotating ball was not solid, it appeared to be made of light. Now he understood why it could float so easily. It was not solid, it was a hologram. An incredibly large hologram. Raymond just lay on the floor marveling at the earth rotating above him. One moment he was lying, staring at the globe, and the next moment he was hearing voices.

10

THEY INTRODUCE THEMSELVES AND THE PLAN FOR HUMANS

Raymond was listening to the voices and realized he could not see anything. Everything felt like a dream. The voices were soft, and gentle, but sounded far away. He tried opening his eyes, but they would not open, he also could not move a muscle. The voices were telling him not to be afraid, he was not in danger. He did not know what was wrong with him, but he felt calm, not worried a bit. The voices told him they were there to help. If he were having dreams, this would be one of the weirdest dreams he had ever had. He felt himself relax even more as the voices talked to him, and explained they were going to let him wake up in a minute, but he needed to try and relax. This was one of the weirdest dreams I have ever had, thought Raymond. The voices finally said, "You can open your eyes, and sit up now Raymond." Once he heard that he was able to open his eyes he knew this was not a dream, but he was a little nervous to sit up and see who was talking. He sat up and turned toward the voices to see who was talking to him. At once, he wished he had not opened his eyes and looked. Standing no more than twenty feet from him, were four of the largest ape-like animals he had ever seen.

Raymond was sure if he had not been sitting down, he would

have started running. He sat there looking at four large furry things and could not move. He could not speak. He was frozen, unable to move, unable to utter a sound. He was not sure if he could breathe. All he was able to do was sit and stare. One of the beings raised its arm and spoke English to him. At this point Raymond was starting to believe he was asleep and having an unbelievably bad nightmare. The creature went on to tell Raymond he was not in any danger; they were here to help him. It told him they had watched over humans and protected them for thousands of years. We built these caverns to protect our species and yours. Thousands of years ago humans stayed in these caverns during disasters that would have wiped them out, it said. There will be a time soon that humans, and our species again will have to inhabit these caverns for protection. We have watched you as you traveled through the cavern these past days, it said. Raymond, you have shown profound respect for the cavern, and everything inside of it during your journey. The choices you made to explore here have shown us humans are ready to join our species in these caverns again. We have studied humans for thousands of years waiting for you to mature, and we believe it is the time to let our presence be known, it said. There is still over a decade before humans will need to move into the caverns, for your safety. I cannot yet reveal what the danger is but soon it will be time. For now, we must remain hidden and silent until the proper time. Before we leave, and let you return to your home, we have a surprise for you.

I believe you have been looking for these people, it said. When it had finished talking, something started to rise out of the floor. A large black shape was slowly rising out of the floor behind the large beings. Once it had completely risen out of the floor Raymond could see it was a huge ship. It was completely black, no windows, three hundred feet long, shaped like a slender spaceship. He guessed it was the same ship he had seen under water in the cavern many times. Even with its incredibly slender shape Raymond could not imagine how it could travel so fast underwater. It looked like it would fly fast but how could it go so fast underwater? While he was staring at the ship a door slid open, and two old men walked out.

Raymond instantly recognized Papa from the pictures, and not only was he alive but he looked great. He was smiling and looked like a man in his sixties, not 110 years old. He had never seen pictures of Kirk, but he assumed that the old man next to Papa was him. Kirk also looked fit and moved like someone much younger than his real age. Papa walked up to Raymond and said, "hello young man." "Thank you for looking for Kirk and me." Raymond was speechless. He had seen so many things he could not explain in the cavern, but this was the most extraordinary. Papa explained he knew exactly who Raymond was, and why he was there. To be honest Raymond, I visit Grandma every night, and I have known about you, since Stella and you moved in years ago. Papa explained how the Sasquatch, which is what they were called, he said, saved Kirk, and I when we fell down the shaft. He said Kirk and he were hurt very badly, but the Sasquatch saved them from death. They were unable to return home because the Sasquatch were not ready to be found out. Now that it is close to the time when the Sasquatch are going to let their presence known, they felt it was time for someone to come down the shaft. Their primary reason was to find out how humans would behave in the caverns. "You pass the test, Raymond," Papa said.

Papa went on to explain how he and Kirk, along with Grandma, have lived so long. The Sasquatch technology is much further advanced than human technology. The plants that grow in this cavern will extend human life to well over one-hundred-fifty years. You can tell by Kirk's and my fitness; I am telling the truth. Grandma has also been eating the food from the cavern which is why she is so healthy. To be honest Raymond, Grandma has been in on this ruse the whole time. She set you up to come down here to search for Kirk and me. Your choices for exploring this cavern have set the Sasquatch minds at ease. They now know humans can co-exist in these caverns peacefully, with ample education of course. "Also, you can expect quite a long lifetime which seeing as you now have quite a large bank account, will be enjoyable," said Papa. "The Sasquatch has one more surprise for you Raymond," he said. When Papa finished talking, the door on the ship opened again. When the door opened, Grandma and Stella walked out. Raymond could not believe his eyes when he saw Stella walk out of the box. He instantly rushed to her and hugged her as she stepped out.

"Raymond," she said, "I am fine, they have explained everything to me, and I understand. We have nothing to worry about."

The Sasquatch stepped forward to speak to Raymond. You and Stella will be going back to your homes as if nothing different has happened. Papa, Kirk and Grandma will be staying with us. It would be unwise for Kirk and Papa to go back into your world at this time. We are not ready to be found out, and they will live long healthy lives down here with us. "You will also be free to visit them anytime you want, and there are times they will be going up to visit you," it said. Don't worry, arrangements have been made so that the humans above will think that Grandma is off visiting, and it is fine. It is also time that human scientists study our technology and our people. We will help you contact certain individuals in government, and the scientific world to that order. Thank you, Raymond, now you and Stella may return to your home, and you are free to visit this cavern anytime you would like. You will be given a device to communicate with us if there is a need. We will also use the device to communicate with you if we need. It is now time for us to leave. Arrangements have been made to take care of the house, and your pets, so that you and Stella may take your time going back down the cavern to the shaft. When the Sasquatch finished talking, it turned around and it and the other Sasquatch walked into the ship.

Grandma stepped up to Raymond and gave him a big hug. "Thank you, Raymond," she said. "I know you have been put through a tough time, but it was a test that needed to be taken, and you passed. Not just for yourself, but for humanity. Now it is time for Kirk, Papa and I to join the Sasquatch." Here is the device you need to contact us, and the Sasquatch will contact you if they need to. Aside from a large bank account, the Sasquatch wanted to reward you by bringing Stella down so that you could both return home together. They also wanted her to enjoy the time in the cavern going back out. There is no hurry to leave the cavern. Every bit of the food you see growing here is edible and extremely healthy. Another side benefit from the food down in the cavern is that you will live an exceptionally long healthy life, said Grandma. She then hugged Stella and Raymond, then said goodbye for now. With that Grandma, Kirk, and Papa turned and walked into the door the Sasquatch had. The giant black ship noiselessly sunk into the floor and disappeared.

Raymond held Stella's hand, standing together and watching the three walk away. "Well Raymond," said Stella, it's time we started our vacation together. Stella and Raymond turned around and walked out of the domed room toward home.

ABOUT THE AUTHOR

Patrick Talmadge Sr. has always been a late bloomer. His growth didn't cease until he was over 21 years old. He reached his pinnacle as a national and world-class masters middle-distance runner at the age of 37, when he won his first master's national track and field championship in the 800-meter run.

At 47, Patrick earned his Bachelor of Arts degree and made history as the oldest NCAA cross-country runner. Seven years later, at 54, he returned to college to pursue a master's degree in psychology. During this time, he ran the mile in track, once again setting a record as the oldest NCAA track and field runner. He received his master's degree in psychology at 57. At the age of 66, he embarked on his writing journey.

Patrick taught himself to read at the tender age of three and a half and has been an avid reader ever since. With a keen interest in all fields of science, science fiction, and fantasy, he amassed a wealth of knowledge that would later prove invaluable when he began writing. Throughout his 20s and 30s, Patrick devoured two to three books a day. Upon graduating from graduate school in 2011, he retired from competitive running and felt a growing desire to write the stories that had been simmering within him.

In November 2021, spurred on by the love of his life, Patrick began his writing career. By July 2023, he had completed an adult four-book science fiction series about Sasquatch, a four-book children's series on the same subject, and a standalone novel about a senior community that befriends a troupe of Sasquatch.

Patrick possesses a unique ability to write multiple stories simultaneously, allowing him to modify and adjust interconnected narratives for clarity when writing a series. With a bit of luck, Patrick will continue to pursue his passion for writing for the rest of his life, or at least until his computer gives out.

ALSO BY PATRICK TALMADGE

Hidden Mountain Chronicles

Sasquatch Race

Sasquatch Prison Diary

Tenino Caverns

Sasquatch Home Planet

Sasquatch Chronicles

Hunter and Noah vs. Sasquatch Vol. 1

Hunter and Noah vs. Sasquatch Vol. 2

Hunter and Noah vs. Sasquatch Vol. 3

Hunter and Noah vs. Sasquatch Vol. 4

Sasquatch Senior Community Series

Sasquatch Senior Community

Sasquatch Senior Community: Lois and Mel the Beginning

Sasquatch Senior Community: The Early Years

Sasquatch Senior Community: The Middle Years

AFTERWORD

Go to hangar1publishing.com to learn more about the Authors and stay up to date with their newest releases.